NO DO[...]

'I don't want a *good* husband, I want a rich, exciting one.' And with that in mind, Jenny Speed, whirlwind Staff Nurse of the Royal's private ward, has sworn never to go out with a member of the medical staff. By coincidence, so has gorgeous orthopaedic consultant, Gerard Sterne . . .

NO DOCTORS, PLEASE

*Books you will enjoy
in our Doctor Nurse series:*

NO DOCTORS, PLEASE

BY

LYDIA BALMAIN

MILLS & BOON LIMITED
15–16 BROOK'S MEWS
LONDON W1A 1DR

*First published in Great Britain 1984
by Mills & Boon Limited*

© Lydia Balmain 1984

*Australian copyright 1985
Philippine copyright 1985*

ISBN 0 265 74932 0

*For Sharon Cunniss,
because she likes them.*

Set in 10 on 12pt Linotron Times
03–0185–53,250

*Photoset by Rowland Phototypesetting Ltd
Bury St Edmunds, Suffolk
Made and printed in Great Britain by
Richard Clay (The Chaucer Press) Ltd
Bungay, Suffolk*

CHAPTER ONE

ALTHOUGH it was mid-afternoon the canteen was crowded, with the staff of the Royal who were taking a tea-break hurrying in to grab a quick cup before returning to duty and those who were displaced by visitors snatching a moment to themselves. Jenny Speed, hurrying into the large, airy room, stopped short for a moment, surprised by the crowd, then spotted her friend Katrina already well up the queue and hastened to join her.

'You can stop saving up to advertise my place in the flat, love!' Jenny grabbed a tray and smiled jubilantly at her friend. 'I shan't have to leave the good old Royal or the flat—I got the job! From Monday I'm staff nurse on the Annabel Goodson Private Ward!'

'That's marvellous,' Katrina Morris said, beaming at her friend. 'How did the interview go? I dare say they asked awkward questions, because the variety of nursing on a private ward means you have to be pretty efficient.'

'It went terribly well. There was a nursing officer, one of the grim, battle-axe types, and Sister Fox—I'll be working with her—and a couple of fellows. One was Mr Hopwood, he's a consultant with lots of private patients, and the other was his registrar.' She rolled her eyes appreciatively. 'He's very dishy—Dr Pierre Mongresin. I expect it was his vote which got me the job, I could see he was taking in every detail of my appearance. He's a man who likes his nurses to look attractive and doesn't worry too much about efficiency, I bet.'

'I can just see a registrar being listened to in that august company! But you'll have got the job on merit, pet. You've passed all your exams with flying colours, you're a damned good nurse and, as the registrar seems to have noticed, you've got the appearance.' Katrina chuckled, leaning forward to look wistfully at the display of cakes. 'It's important on a private ward to appoint a nurse who also looks every inch a lady.'

She eyed her friend affectionately as Jenny selected two of the largest currant buns. Jenny had long, pale blonde hair, flawless skin and the most surprising eyes—big and sherry-coloured where one expected blue or grey. She had an exquisitely proportioned figure and the fact that she had worked for a year as a model before going into nursing was no doubt the reason she held herself so beautifully, with a poise which few other members of her chosen profession could rival. However, at Katrina's words she chuckled and turned to smile at her friend.

'Looks can be very deceiving, though! Wait until they hear me arguing or getting shrill, then they'll wish they had been careful and hadn't gone by appearances. Here, I'll treat you to a dish of strawberry ice, to celebrate—or are you still on a diet?'

'I'm always on a diet,' Katrina said gloomily. 'Especially with summer galloping up. May usually sees me starting a diet, and this May is no exception. I'm going to Majorca with Tessie and she's thin as a lathe. When I think of her bottom and mine reclining side by side on the beach I immediately forbear starch. Only just this once, as we're celebrating your job, I'll have a currant bun, to keep you company.'

They reached the end of the counter where a harassed

woman in a gingham overall was dispensing tea. Jenny smiled at her.

'Afternoon, Dot. Guess who's going to start work on the Annabel Goodson ward on Monday morning?'

'Well done, ducks.' Dot, without being asked, reached behind her for two thick, earthenware mugs instead of the smaller cups. 'One each?'

'Yes, please, both unsugared,' Jenny said. She swept their tray up to the cash register. 'Hello, Edie, guess who . . .'

'I heard.' The skinny old lady snapped her glasses further down her nose and peered over the top of them at the two trays. 'Take 'em together, shall I, since you'll be in the money, Monday?'

'Yes, I'm treating this worthless girl to her tea.' Jenny, with a lordly gesture, reached for her purse, then yelped as Edie rang up the total. 'I'm a staff nurse, Edie, not a millionaire—though I sincerely trust that I'll either inherit or marry money, working amongst all the idle rich up in the private ward.'

'You don't want to say things like that,' Edie reproved, taking the money and pushing the till shut with a clatter. 'They want little ladies in Annabel Goodson.'

'Ye gods, everyone's got the same impression,' Jenny groaned, as they settled themselves at a small table for two in the window. 'I popped my head into ENT as I came back from the interview and Mandy was there. She said more or less the same thing! Never mind, at least I'll be paying my whack at the end of the month.' She picked up her first bun and bit into it. 'A thousand quid more is not to be sneezed at!'

Katrina smiled. She knew well enough that Jenny had not enjoyed being the only one of the four girls who shared the flat in Byron Road not yet on the staff and consequently on a student's salary. Two years ago, when they had joined forces, only Katrina herself had been fully qualified, but since then both Mandy Crewe and Helen Beckwith had obtained SRN status and a job to go with it. Now that she would be paying her full share of the rent, she guessed Jenny would feel very much better about her much-loved fourth share in the small flat.

'As long as you don't expect extra privileges to go with your rent increase. Did you get shown round the ward, or is that a treat in store?'

'No, they're saving that for Monday. I went into Sister's office and through their little reception hall— that's nice, I must say. A bowl of tulips on a low table and heaps of new magazines—*Vogue*, *Country Life*, all very upper!'

'It's things like that that they pay for, I suppose.' Katrina finished her bun and pushed her chair back from the table. 'I'm off now, love, but many congrats. I'm more glad than I can say. The four of us get on so well that we all dreaded losing you and perhaps getting someone who didn't fit in. What are you doing this evening? I'll be home, and so will Helen, so perhaps we could celebrate with something a bit more substantial than tea and buns.'

'I'm coming as well,' Jenny said, hastily draining her cup. 'I kept hoping that even if I couldn't get in here, I'd make St Cecilia's or one of the other hospitals nearby. That's one thing about central London, there are job opportunities if you've got somewhere to live. But it wouldn't have been the same, it's much better the way it is.'

'True. Are you going back to the ward, or are you off for the rest of the day?'

'I took a day off, so I'm going back to the flat where I'll soak in a hot bath and then put on my nicest frock and take you all out for a meal with the cash I got for the Saturday job.'

'Smashing. Are you sure Mandy isn't going out with someone, though?'

'She is later, but she said she'd come for a celebratory meal first.'

'Right.' Katrina paused at the end of the corridor leading to her ward. 'Are you going to take on that Saturday job again? I know you gave it up so that you could study for the exam, but now . . .'

'No, I quit and I'm going to stay quit. Anyway, they don't really want me at this time of year, they need models most towards Christmas.' Jenny, to everyone's envy, had modelled clothes on Saturday mornings for the coffee-drinkers at a nearby store. 'Anyway, it was rotten not being able to get back to see my mother and now I should be able to manage with the bigger salary, plus all our little extras.' She turned towards the plate glass doors which led out into the short drive. 'See you tonight then, Kat!'

Making her way through the visitors thronging out into the bright May afternoon, Jenny reflected that though their flat had its disadvantages, it had one useful factor. It was situated over a very noisy amusement arcade, which meant that the rent was a good deal lower than it would otherwise have been, and the girls were very much in demand to do the odd night's work in the change booth, sitting behind little piles of fifty, ten and five pence pieces and towers of coppers, giving change to any patron who might need it. This meant that anyone in desperate need of a bit extra could usually earn it without having to go far from home.

There were disadvantages, of course. If one came home late and alone, sometimes one had to run a gauntlet of idlers or young idiots who thought it funny to accost a nurse who was only wanting to get home and into bed. The noise, too, during the evenings meant that closing time could not come soon enough when one just wanted to sleep. But after two years the four of them were wise to most of the snags. If you came home late and in uniform, a phone call first to the manager of the arcade would ensure that either Vince himself or Jimmy or Ralph, the chuckers-out, would be hovering, glad to escort you safely into the flat. But mostly, the girls found they could cope very well themselves. Jenny in particular, with her stunning looks and her quick wits, could usually make her way up to the flat without parrying anything more than comments.

Parents, of course, did not take kindly to the location of the flat. But Jenny's mother, widowed and sixty years old next January, had always been broadminded and very partisan towards her daughter.

'She's been well brought up, so no photographer will tempt her to act foolishly,' she had said tartly to a neighbour who had wondered aloud at Mrs Speed allowing her young daughter to model.

'It's unusual, but it's cheap and clean,' she had said equally tartly to Katrina's mother, when they had first visited the flat. 'My Jennifer can take care of herself. Doubtless you trust Katrina to do the same.'

This brisk attitude had saved the girls a lot of trouble, and Jenny mentally saluted her mother as she climbed the stairs towards the flat. Mrs Speed ran a small boutique in Bath, specialising in good but very expensive clothing and, dearly though she loved Jenny, she was an independent woman who intended to remain so.

'We won't interfere with each other, dear,' she had remarked when Jenny first left school and announced that she wanted to go to London to find out what life was all about. 'That way, we'll remain friends.'

They had. Sometimes it was on the tip of Jenny's tongue to ask Mrs Speed when she intended to retire, to suggest that she looked tired after a full Saturday serving in the shop. Always the words were bitten back, unsaid. Sharper than a serpent's tooth might be an ungrateful child, ran her thoughts, but how much worse a nagging one!

Jenny let herself into the flat, closed the door behind her, and went through to the living-room, flooded by afternoon sunshine. She would ring home now and tell her news, then she would have a bath and put on her scarlet and white dress. She had got it very cheaply after a customer had spilt coffee over the skirt, but a good wash had soon cured that and the dress looked expensive and special.

The phone call was short because Mrs Speed was working, but she was thrilled with Jenny's news and urged her daughter to come home soon so that they could talk about her new job at length.

'I'm working this Saturday, but I'm off the following one,' she assured Jenny. 'So we could have a nice long day together, though you'd have to amuse yourself on the Sunday; Uncle Bob's taking me out for the day.'

Jenny promised to return home as soon as she could, though she foresaw that there would be plenty to learn on her new ward and knew that she would be working three weekends out of four. However, Mrs Speed understood the difficulties of getting time off from a new job, so one way and another they would work things out.

After the telephone call Jenny laid out her clean clothes, polished a pair of white court shoes and went and ran her bath. She would have a nice, long soak, she planned, undressing and pushing her uniform into the linen bag which hung behind the bathroom door. Uniforms were laundered at the hospital, thank goodness, and anyway she would be needing a new one. Staff nurses wore lilac coloured dresses with dark purple belts, and she was looking forward to fitting the antique silver buckle her mother had given her to celebrate the passing of her exams on to the new belt. She climbed into the hot water and sighed. She had a job!

'There are a good few rooms, as you can see, Nurse, twenty in all. We take private patients from all the consultants but because of the obvious difficulties with orthopaedic patients, Mr Sterne's people go into the first few rooms, usually, and the others we fit in where we can. There are two double rooms, we call them amenity beds, which are used if patients want company or if we're very full. You'll find that Mr Hopwood and Mr Sterne provide most of our patients, but of course other consultants do send people in from time to time.'

Sister Fox, a pretty, dark-haired girl in her mid-twenties, was about to take Jenny for a tour of her new domain. Jenny was interested to see that it was all rather similar to any other ward really, apart from the private rooms, which made nursing more difficult. But the kitchen, the sluice, the linen cupboard and even Sister's office were very similar to those she had been using for the past three years.

'I've met Mr Hopwood, but I can't remember Mr Sterne,' Jenny said thoughtfully. 'I did orthopaedics but it was during the flu epidemic, so I may have missed him. Mr Hopwood's got a white moustache, hasn't he? He was on the interview board.'

'That's right. Tall chap. Mr Sterne's tall too, but a good deal younger and very dark haired. He's got a sarcastic tongue and he can let rip if you make mistakes, but he's a first-rate surgeon.'

'I'll try not to make mistakes then,' Jenny said. 'Are procedures very different here, Sister, from other wards? There must be drug rounds and charts on the beds and so on, but a bedpan round sounds rather *infra dig*!'

Sister laughed.

'Yes, procedures are very similar, even to getting the patients up at ungodly hours. But try to remember that the patients are paying enormous sums of money for our attention, and never let a patient call or ring for a moment longer than necessary. Also, the patient is very much the boss. If they decide to walk out there's nothing we can do about it and it would be very bad for our image. So no matter how trying a patient is, we have to be understanding and sympathetic.' She smiled at the younger girl. 'Do you know what it costs someone just to stay here, without even counting surgeon's fees, anaesthetist's fees and so on?'

Jenny shook her head and Sister Fox named an astronomical sum which made Jenny blink. Sister Fox laughed.

'Yes, it sounds a lot—well, it is a lot! But the money goes towards the general running of the hospital as well as that of this ward and the way I see it, if people want to pay for privacy and a degree of special attention, it helps the National Health to pay for absolute essentials, special equipment and so on. To say nothing of our wages!'

'Yes, I see that. I've heard nurses grumbling about private patients, saying that they keep you on the run all day, but Sister Tutor used to say that it was the best type of ward to get your experience on because you'd nurse so many different types of ailments and accidents. And I suppose you meet some pretty interesting people, too.'

'That's true. Then shall we do the rounds? The ward isn't full but it will be by the end of the week, though we get quite a few short-stay patients, partly for financial reasons, of course.'

They left the office and walked down the long corridor, but outside Room One Sister came to a halt, her hand resting on the door handle. 'I should have said that we get famous people in here sometimes and once in a while you'll see a face you recognise attached to a name you don't. If they're here for peace and quiet they don't want everyone to know who they are, so you have to learn discretion. Others want to be recognised and enjoy nursely adulation, but again, you'll soon learn where to draw the line.'

Jenny peered at the door. There was a slot into which a name could be fed; this one read simply, *Mr Preedy*. She raised her brows at Sister.

'What about this one? Is he someone else?'

Sister chuckled. 'We-ell, see if you recognise him.' She opened the door and the two of them entered the luxuriously furnished room. 'Good morning, Mr Preedy, did you have a good night?'

The man in the bed was tall and thin, judging from the position of his feet beneath the covers. He was also very young, no more than twenty, Jenny thought, and his hair had been cropped very short at the back and sides and left rather long at the top. It had been dyed first a brilliant shade of Jaffa-orange and then the ends had, it appeared, been dipped in yellow ochre. He swivelled deep-set, almost black eyes towards them as they entered and a smile lit up his rather angular face.

'Morning, Sister!' His eyes brightened as they fell on Jenny and a hand strayed to the strange hair and then down again, to tug at a cream silk pyjama jacket. 'Oh, a stranger, I see! Morning, Nurse!'

'Good morning, Mr Preedy,' Jenny said demurely. She went over to his bed and took out the thermometer which was kept in a small holder above it. 'Shall I do observation, Sister?'

'Please. Mr Preedy will be here for another week to ten days, but we check his temperature, pulse and blood pressure regularly.'

Jenny was an efficient nurse, though in this case the patient was none too helpful—for in his attempts to watch her as she worked, he kept getting entangled in the sheets and in her equipment. By the time she left the room, indeed, Jenny had hard work not to laugh, and outside the door, turned at once to Sister.

'That was Alvin, the pop-singer, wasn't it? What's the matter with him? He seemed pretty healthy to me.'

'He is now. A week ago he was in a poor way. Overdose.'

'Dear me, I shouldn't have thought he was the type,' Jenny said mildly. 'What was it, some girl who wouldn't when he thought she should?'

'Nothing like that. The young man's too fond of himself to deliberately do any harm. No, he was at a party, having had a good deal to drink, when someone started handing round pills—drugs, anyway. He helped himself liberally and that was the last he remembered. He came into Casualty and was in Cheshire on intensive care for a week, but as soon as he was fit enough he asked for a private room, so we're lumbered with him.'

'Is he very trying? He looks pretty weedy and harmless without his make-up and sequins.'

'He is—both harmless and trying, I suppose. He's convinced he's a big star and whenever he hears footsteps in the corridor he rings for a nurse and says autograph-hunters are after him. And when he isn't doing that, he's fussing about all the engagements he's missing and ringing his agent and trying to get my staff to take dictation. He's driven my girls mad, particularly over the weekend.'

'I've only seen him once, on *Top of the Pops*, and I probably wouldn't have recognised him if it hadn't been for that hair and those slightly mad eyes,' Jenny confessed. 'What are we doing for him?'

'We're building him up. He has taken quite a knock, and we do a blood sample each day because his count's low. That'll fall to you, and I don't envy you. He has a horror of needles.'

'I'll survive,' Jenny said. 'But I wonder if Alvin will?'

'We've got a lot of characters, I'll say that for 'em,' Jenny remarked later that day as she and Katrina ate a salad in the canteen. 'We've got Alvin Preedy, that pop-star with the orange hair we saw a week or so ago on *Top of the Pops*. I had to take a blood sample from him. You've never seen anything like the fuss he made, went all through the old agony routine! I'm a jolly good blood-letter, I don't think he felt a thing, so it was all anticipation. I got cold and exasperated, which is the nearest I dare get to bawling a private patient out!'

'What about the others? Are they terribly demanding? That's what they say.'

'Some are, some aren't. There's an old terror who came in today for a hip replacement on Thursday. She's called Miss Stott and she's going to drive everyone mad, I can guess that. And there's a severe back-pain who's on traction at the moment—that's Mrs Franklyn. She's thin and demanding, with half-moon glasses and a voice which carries rather too well for my liking. I wouldn't be surprised if she turned out to have been a prison wardress or a matron before she retired.'

'Yes, I see the connection,' Katrina said, eating tinned pilchards. 'What about the rest of the staff? I know all about Sister Fox, but what about the others?'

'Well, we've got two SENs, Pat Roach and Gillian Black. They're great, Pat's in her late twenties and Gill's about my age, and they're both so tactful and sensible that they make me feel callow. And there are three maids, but I've only met one so far, Doreen. She's nice as well. They seem a decent lot. Oh, and we've *two* film-stars, no less, only I'm not supposed to talk about them in case you come rushing up with your autograph book.'

Katrina laughed. 'Don't worry, I shan't give you away. Who are they?'

'Well, one calls herself Mrs Widdowes. Perhaps that's her real name, come to think, and she's Elsa Lamour— do you remember seeing her in *Love's A Laugh*? And the other's Morna Lane. She must be sixty, you see her films on telly sometimes.'

'Gosh! Is Elsa as lovely as she looked on the screen?'

'Yes, she's pretty striking, though she bleaches her hair and wears false eyelashes.' Jenny finished her salad and glanced up at the canteen clock. 'I'd better head for the hills, I've got a ward round with Mr Sterne, he's the one I haven't met yet, at two o'clock, so I don't want to be late for that.'

'You've not met Gerard Sterne? A treat in store, my child!'

Jenny pulled a face. 'With a name like that? Bye, Kat, see you tonight!'

Arriving, breathless, back on the ward, Jenny was just in time to see the light above Mrs Franklyn's door glow scarlet. She glanced round but neither of the SENs were in sight, though Pat had a late lunch today, so she made for Room Eight.

As she entered, she glanced at her watch. It was one-thirty, so by rights the ward round should not start for another half-hour, but Sister had implied that Mr Sterne was more often early than late, so she must see to Mrs Franklyn quickly and get back to the office.

Her patient was lying flat, since she was on traction for her back-pain, and at first glance all seemed in order, though her expression was forbidding. At second glance, Jenny saw the plate of food congealing on the side-table, apparently untouched. She hurried to the bedside.

'You rang, Mrs Franklyn? Why haven't you eaten your fish?'

'Because I never touch fish; never have. The girl brought it and I waited for her to return with something more acceptable, but she has failed to do so.' She turned her head so that Jenny might get the full effect of her annoyance. 'I wish for a decent meal, not this—this . . . pap!'

Jenny took the plate and looked at the fish. It was white, steamed, with two hard-looking boiled potatoes flanking it and parsley sauce in a puddle at one side. Not appetising now, perhaps, when stone-cold, but it had probably been reasonable enough, as steamed fish went, an hour earlier.

'Yes, I see—you aren't on a diet, are you?'

'Certainly not! What is more, Nurse, I did expect some sort of choice—that was what I had been led to believe!'

'And what you'll get, for dinner this evening,' Jenny assured her, crossing her fingers behind her back. 'The thing is, Mrs Franklyn, you came in at eleven and by then the menus had all gone back to the canteen. So new patients get no choice for their first meal.'

'Well, I want you to take this back, Nurse,' Mrs Franklyn said. 'I'd like a piece of liver, lightly grilled, with duchesse potatoes and a few peas. Oh, and gravy of course. And then I'll have some strawberry blancmange.'

'I don't imagine that will be possible,' Jenny said apologetically. 'The staff probably don't have liver just waiting to be grilled, and . . .'

'I am *not* in my dotage; that is the meal which Miss Stott was given. She is still able to walk around, and she came in here to enquire whether I had had my meal and told me what she had just eaten.'

'Oh, in that case I could take this back to the kitchens and see if they've any liver left. Tell me, Mrs Franklyn, why did you wait so long? I'm sure someone else could have taken it down for you.'

'I rang once, and then waited. Miss Stott and I have quite a lot in common, we were both in the same profession, and we began to chat. Time slipped away, I suppose.' Mrs Franklyn sighed and turned her head rather fretfully on the pillow. 'Please hurry, Nurse. I'm really extremely hungry.'

'I'll be as quick as I can,' Jenny said, taking the

despised main course on its tray, together with an anonymous pudding beneath a metal cover. 'But if all the liver's gone, will you have some other meat?'

'I suppose so.'

Jenny hurried off out of the ward, thinking vengefully that it was just like Miss Stott to go interfering. Wretched old woman, no wonder Sister had said that they did not encourage the patients to visit each other's private rooms but told them instead to congregate in the waiting-room if they were feeling sociable. But still, the damage had been done, and now she must do her best to put it right!

Once in the kitchens, she stood diffidently by the door, glancing at the staff, all of whom seemed engaged, at that moment, in clearing up, until a cook approached her. She was an elderly woman with a flushed face and spiky grey hair, on top of which was perched an unflattering cap. It looked a bit like a pudding-cloth.

'Yes?'

'Oh, it's about this fish. The patient's new in today and she can't touch fish, and I wondered . . .'

'Which ward? Any diet given?'

The words, snapped out, did nothing for Jenny's self-confidence. *Had* there been a diet for the patient? But she thought not, and Mrs Franklyn had been very definite on that score.

'Er . . . Annabel Goodson Ward, and no diet I don't think, but wouldn't it be on the ward's menus?'

'Yes, but I'm not looking through that lot.' The woman snatched the plate out of Jenny's grasp and turned to a huge oven, swinging the door back impatiently. 'Well? There's some macaroni cheese and some fish.'

'No liver? She fancied the liver, apparently.'

The cook heaved another sigh and cast a look of burning contempt at poor Jenny.

'Oh, *fancied* it, did she? Couldn't say, of course, when the girl took the fish in?'

'She's on traction; I dare say she didn't look under the cover at the time,' Jenny said mendaciously. 'Is there any liver?'

The cook did not reply but fished in the back of the oven, producing a very tiny, hard-looking piece of liver alone on a plate. She held it out, then scooped the boiled potatoes off the fish plate and on to the liver one. She then proffered the bald-looking plate to Jenny.

Jenny took a deep breath. Who does this woman think she is? she thought crossly. I will *not* let her scare me away with that—and if I do, I'll have to face Mrs Franklyn!

'The liver should have gravy, duchesse potatoes and peas,' she said firmly. 'Would you put them on the plate for me, please?'

The cook grabbed a fork, battered the boiled potatoes into some sort of lumpy submission, sloshed cooling, greyish gravy all over them and added a teaspoonful of dried up little peas.

'Satisfied, madam?'

'No, but if it's the best you can do, I'll just have a helping of strawberry blancmange to replace this . . .' Jenny lifted the cover and saw that it contained runny rice pudding, '. . . this stuff.'

The choleric cook, her high colour heightened by Jenny's calmness, snorted, took the rice pudding and went over to a table near the door where several large bowls stood. She ladled out a helping of the blancmange and then slapped it down—hard—on Jenny's outstretched tray.

'Nurses! They're worse than patients, if you ask me!'

'Oh, I do agree!' Jenny gave her the benefit of her most charming smile. 'By the way, cook, I've been longing to ask you—*is* that a pudding-cloth on your head?'

She escaped while the cook was still gibbering and hurried up the stairs, hoping devoutly that she had no cause to visit the kitchens for another ten years or so.

As she reached the foyer of the ward, a quick glance at the clock confirmed that she stood a good chance of being late for Mr Sterne's round. Jenny groaned, but duty was duty, and she *had* been working on a patient's behalf, so she hurried along the corridor, the tray of food held out before her. As she passed Room Two, the door shot open and the surgeon and his team emerged. Mr Sterne had his head turned and was addressing the man nearest him and naturally, he collided with considerable force with Jenny's extended tray.

He was just in time, as he turned his head, to see the gravy, which had not halted as quickly as Jenny, slurp from the plate and land unerringly on his black, highly polished shoes. Jenny, mesmerised by its downward flight, could only stare at the shoes, and the fawn-coloured puddle now adorning each gleaming toecap.

'Ah, Sister, a new kitchen maid, I see. Why on earth is she in staff nurse uniform?'

His voice was deep and might have been quite pleasant had it not been so heavily laden with sarcasm. Jenny tore her gaze from his shoes and looked up . . . and up. He was very tall, and as dark as Sister had said, but now he looked far from handsome, with the thick brows raised and a sardonic smile on his mouth.

'This is Nurse Speed, Mr Sterne.'

Sister's voice was non-committal, but she gave Jenny a reassuring glance. Anyone can make mistakes, that glance said. Mr Sterne, however, obviously felt he had good mileage still to come out of her foolishness.

'Speed? Yes, she was exhibiting a rare turn of speed.' He glanced closely at the plate of liver. 'Is this someone's vital organ? Is that why you were rushing?'

Dutiful titters from his team did nothing to help Jenny's blushes, but she did not intend to allow such facetious remarks to go unchallenged. She gave him a serious look.

'Yes. I'm afraid this particular patient died.' For the life of her she could not have stopped the next words following, though she knew she would regret them. Limpidly, she continued to look up at him. 'Lamb, sir—was he one of yours?'

He stared down at her for an unnerving moment, during which thoughts of immediate suicide following being sacked within five hours of starting her first job flashed through Jenny's mind. Then he grinned.

'Quite a wit! No, I'm not a veterinary surgeon, but we're just about to visit one. If you'll go and get a cloth I'll get this gunge off my shoes and go on with my round.' His smile seemed genuine now, and genuinely amused, too. 'You might like to accompany us, Staff.'

'Oh, I would, I would,' Jenny gabbled, relief flooding through her. Her wretched tongue had not alienated him completely, then! She thrust the tray into the hands of a nearby doctor and dropped to her knees, feverishly mopping gravy with her handkerchief. 'There you are, sir, as good as new!'

She jumped to her feet, snatching the tray back from the surprised doctor, making everyone flinch defensively back as the gravy swirled sluggishly once more. 'This is Mrs Franklyn's lunch. I'll just take it along to her, I shan't be a sec.'

However, Mr Sterne was not to be so easily dismissed. As she went to pass him a hand caught her shoulder, holding her firmly.

'Just a moment, Nurse. It's a quarter to two, what are you doing, bringing patients their lunches well over an hour late? It's not your job.'

'Well, no, sir, but the lady's a new admission and they brought her fish, which she doesn't eat. She asked me to change it for her, and . . .'

'You should have phoned down, Nurse, not gone racing off to the kitchens yourself.' He shook his head reprovingly, quite grave now. 'Suppose a patient had a fall, or haemorrhaged? A kitchen girl wouldn't be much good, the patient would need a nurse.'

'Oh!' It had not occurred to her to ring down. On a busy ward, it was usual to despatch the most junior nurse on errands of that kind, and until this very morning she herself had usually been the most junior nurse in sight! She sighed, then looked straight up at him. 'I'm sorry, sir, I didn't think.'

'I see you do understand. Another time, ring down to the kitchens and get them to send up a replacement.' He smiled briefly at her. 'I'm afraid the patients on Annabel Goodson are sometimes rather fussy about their meals.' He flicked the tray with a forefinger. 'And judging by the appearance of that liver, not without reason. Is that really the best the cook could do? Very well, Nurse, take it to the patient; we'll wait here.'

'Right away, sir,' Jenny said, setting off at a trot and quickly slowing to a fast walk as, behind her, a throat cleared warningly. She hurried into Mrs Franklyn's room and put the tray down in front of her patient. Mrs

Franklyn's head shot forward like a tortoise peering out of its shell, and her eyes scanned the food.

'Nurse, that liver looks very overcooked and if the kitchen staff call those duchesse potatoes . . .'

'I'm very sorry, it was all they had left,' Jenny said, leaving the room whilst Mrs Franklyn was still preparing her new grumble. She hurried back to where the team were just filing into Room Four and took her place near Sister. She glanced towards the bed, to refresh her memory. Ah, yes, Mr Robert Anderson, age twenty-three, with a fractured tibia which refused to heal. A rugger player and . . . a quick glance at his notes in Sister's hand refreshed her memory, though the surgeon had already mentioned it. Veterinary surgeon—or he would be, if he passed his exams.

'Well, Mr Anderson, tomorrow's the great day, eh?' Mr Sterne turned to his team. 'We're going to give this young man a bone graft tomorrow, get this wretched fracture to knit. I'm going to take bone chippings from the iliac crest and pack them round the fracture, then we'll sew up the wound with six to eight stitches, I suspect.' He turned to the group. 'Next step, someone? Yes, you, the waitress.'

Jenny, who had hoped not to be noticed, gave the surgeon an affronted glare. She had been looking intelligent and keen, but that did not mean she felt up to answering questions! Nevertheless, if she could prove that she knew the right answer, it would go a long way towards correcting the bad impression she must have made, and might even kill the horrors of being nick-named 'the waitress' at birth.

'You'll cover the wound with a below-knee plaster,' she said firmly. 'And there will be a porto-vac drain in the hip, probably for about forty-eight hours. It will be removed then, or when fifty millilitres have been drained off.'

Mr Sterne looked surprised but gratified.

'That's right. Have I misjudged you, Nurse? Well, carry on.'

'Er . . . We elevate the bed so that the limb doesn't swell, and we keep a watch on the toes to see they don't either swell or turn blue, and on the plaster to see that there isn't undue blood seepage,' Jenny said, racking her brain for more. 'The stitches usually come out at ten to fourteen days. A window is cut in the plaster for suture removal and then put back in again, very firmly, until the plaster can come right off. The patient is usually discharged before then, and comes back to the ward for plaster removal and final discharge.'

'Well done, Staff.' She was immensely relieved to note that the sarcasm had gone from his voice as well as his face. 'Although I can't remember seeing you on the general ward, it seems you've got your orthopaedics taped.' He turned to his patient, pretending not to see Sister beaming at Jenny. 'Well, Anderson? When did you break that leg?'

'Last October, sir, playing rugger—nearly seven months ago. I just hope this operation does the trick.'

'Of course it will, though I won't pretend the next few days will be a picnic.' He picked up a book from the bedside table. 'What are you reading?'

The young man grinned.

'Medicine, sir. My veterinary finals are in a month, that's why I elected to come in privately. I didn't dare let my studying lapse.'

'Hmm, I did wonder. Fellows of your age usually prefer the open ward.'

'So I would've, sir, except for the work load, which

I doubt I could manage without a good deal of time to myself.' He grinned up at Jenny. 'The first thing I'll want when I come round after the op will be my books, and if I can't read 'em myself, I'll expect you nurses to read 'em for me!'

'Staff will enjoy reading to you,' Mr Sterne said magnanimously. 'Give her a break from throwing gravy at consultants.' Mr Anderson looked puzzled but the rest of the team grinned, only Jenny feeling that the joke had long gone stale.

They left Mr Anderson studying and passed by Room Six, where a Mr McRae was awaiting a hernia operation the following day, but in Room Eight the first thing the consultant saw was the plate of cold and unappetising food. A hand went up to his mouth for a second, and then he strolled over to the bed and spoke.

'How's the back, Mrs Franklyn? Is the pelvic traction helping? Though I expect it's a bit too . . .'

'Ah, Gerard!' Mrs Franklyn fixed him with a steely eye and to Jenny's joy the great man stepped back. 'The food at this place beggars description! I was clearly told that I might move from my present abject position and on to my side in order to eat, but look at that plate!'

Mr Sterne gave a cursory glance at the plate.

'Yes, I seem to recognise it! Now, Mrs Fra . . .'

'Recognise it?' Mrs Franklyn gave a short bark of amusement. 'Yes, that wouldn't surprise me, I dare say the dining-room staff serve this up regularly, knowing that it will be rejected and offered to the next unhappy victim, like a British Rail sandwich! It won't do, Gerard. When one is lying flat, with a miserable corset pinching one's . . . pinching one, food is eagerly awaited.' She gestured to the tray. 'Imagine my disappointment when I saw that!'

Jenny waited for Mrs Franklyn to be blasted by surgical wrath, but instead, Mr Sterne looked suitably abashed and turned to Sandra Fox, hovering by his elbow. 'Sister?'

'I'm very sorry, Mrs Franklyn. I'm afraid it's one of the anomalies of the present system that the kitchen staff seem unable to provide a decent meal for the first day in hospital. But I assure you that I'll see you get what you'll enjoy this evening.'

'Hmm. I accept your word, Sister.' Mrs Franklyn turned a reproving frown on to Mr Sterne, however. 'The Sister has explained what your little nurse told me, but though I won't tell you how to run your hospital, Gerard, you've known about my dislike of fish for many years. You really should think, my boy. As I used to tell you, always think before you act!'

As her admonitory tone softened, so Jenny's grin broadened. If Mr Sterne dared to refer to her as kitchen maid or waitress again she would jolly well call him Gerard diddums! Who *was* Mrs Franklyn? Could she once have been the consultant's nanny?

She was soon to know. Having done his best to reassure his patient that the hospital was being as properly run as he could manage, Mr Sterne led the rout—and it could not be otherwise described—out of Mrs Franklyn's room and into the corridor, where he turned to his team.

'Sorry about that, but Mrs Franklyn is rather a special case. She was employed by my parents when I was young to teach me French and then, when I was at prep school, she was teaching French there and, well, she's quite a character.' He added, a little self-consciously, 'I did know she was on the ward, of course, but I'd forgotten.' He grinned at them. 'I also forgot how

'. . . how dictatorial she can be, but she's a good sort, underneath that rather forbidding exterior.'

Having done his explaining, he continued with his round and when it finished, Jenny thought that she would escape and lick her wounds in private for a few moments. But to her surprise the surgeon went into Sister's office, from which sanctum he presently sent Sister with a message.

'You're to go the office, Jenny,' Sister said rather apologetically. 'Don't worry, I think he feels he was a bit unfair, not realising what an extraordinarily powerful personality had sent you scuttling off to the kitchens! But you took absolutely the right attitude, you stood up to him, laughed at him a bit, and then managed to answer his questions far better than he would have expected from a nurse who's not done much ortho-paedics. After all, if he can't stand up to his old teacher, he can scarcely expect you to do so! So keep up that attitude that you're willing to be taught but not to be laughed at.'

Entering Sister's office, therefore, Jenny went in boldly and looked straight into Mr Sterne's dark eyes.

'Yes, sir? You sent for me.'

'I did.' He frowned at her, not crossly but intently. 'Haven't I seen you somewhere before, Nurse Speed?'

'That's a familiar line,' Jenny said involuntarily, and was relieved when he smiled. She realised for the first time that Mr Sterne was younger than most consultants; he could not be more than thirty-one or two, and he was a very attractive man into the bargain.

'Yes, it's a time-honoured approach, though I didn't intend it as such,' he agreed. 'Genuinely, your face is familiar. Have you nursed on one of my other wards?'

'No, sir, or at least, not when you were there.' Jenny

hesitated. She knew quite well why it was that her face seemed familiar to him, since that same face was, at the moment, decorating an airline advertisement in the local underground station. Even the uniform of an airline stewardess helped people to recognise her, since it was a little like that of a nurse. However, she did not intend to tell Mr Sterne about her modelling career. One could never tell how a member of the medical profession—and her boss, into the bargain—might take the news. Some said sarcastically that she would regret the change in terms of salary, others that she must have got a very wrong impression of nursing if she thought it a more glamorous career than modelling. Others still assumed, totally mistakenly, that she had joined the profession in order to marry a doctor. Jenny, whose aim in life was never to go out with a member of the medical profession, thought that this was the silliest idea of all, so she rarely mentioned her modelling career at work. Certainly only her closest friends knew that she still took modelling jobs from time to time.

'Odd! You can't think of any other sphere where we might have met?'

He was looking at her searchingly, but she shook her head.

'No, unless it was just around the hospital. I did my training here.'

'Hmm, probably. Ever considered private nursing?' His eyes swept her shrewdly. 'No, of course you haven't, you've only just qualified, but I wondered what made you apply for the Annabel Goodson?'

'Variety of experience and the fact that I wanted to stay at the Royal,' Jenny said. 'Jobs aren't as easy to come by as they were, but I'm not afraid of hard work and I enjoy being with people. And this ward has a reputation for stretching the nurses and for being friendly. And the patients are awfully interesting.' She smiled demurely at him. 'Even the crabby ones.'

'Hmm. Oh, by the way, don't you come from Bath?'

'Yes, sir.'

'Go back often?'

'Well, not every night. I share a flat quite near the hospital, but I spend my holidays in Bath, usually, despite the influx of Americans swarming in to see where the Romans used to live. I'm going back this weekend, actually, so that my mother and I can gossip about my new job.'

'Then that may well be where I've seen you—I'm from Bath myself. I'm going back this weekend, too. Friday evening, actually. Like a lift?'

There was nothing that Jenny wanted less than a lift from a man several years her senior and several miles above her in the hospital hierarchy, but she could only smile, murmur her thanks, and hope that in the intervening four days he would forget the invitation.

'Very well, that's all, Nurse. And don't forget, you're a fully-fledged staff nurse now, not a little student who can be sent off on any convenient errand. Be firm with the patients, though very polite, of course. Don't let any of them, not even a woman with as powerful a personality as my Mrs Franklyn, ride roughshod over you. In other words, no more waitressing!'

He meant it kindly and amusingly no doubt, Jenny told herself as she left the office and hurried in the direction of the red light flashing outside Room Three, but she did hope it was the last time he would use the word 'waitressing' in connection with her activities!

CHAPTER TWO

JENNY HAD a hectic week on the ward, but she was good at her job and soon learned how best to handle her patients.

'It's a blend of friendliness and firmness,' Sandra Fox had said when they discussed their work. 'You've got to be friendly without being too familiar, because some of them are very important people in their own right. Yet you can't let them bully you, or your work as a nurse will suffer. If someone becomes too much for you to handle, the intelligent thing is to admit it and to fetch me, or one of the doctors. Don't wait until the patient thinks he's got the upper hand. Look at Alvin—you did just the right thing there.'

Alvin had got 'out of hand' as Sister called it, on Jenny's third day on the ward. He had rung for her during that period of the afternoon when the patients were supposed to either take a nap or lie on their beds and read, and she had gone, unsuspecting, into his room to find him supine and languid on the chair by the window.

'Hello, lovely,' he said, perking up a little as she crossed the room. 'Come and open this window, would you? I've given it a good jerk but I can't move it.'

'Jerking won't help, Mr Preedy,' Jenny said. She had gone up to the window, which necessitated leaning across his outstretched legs, and had begun to coax it upwards, knowing from past experience with hospital sashes that this was the right approach.

It was actually ascending nicely when Alvin pulled her on to his lap. Jenny laughed, which was a mistake, since Alvin leapt to the conclusion that she was concurring with his behaviour, and then tried to get up, whereupon he put his arms round her, swung her half on to her back and proceeded to kiss her with fervour, proving, as she told Sister later, how very much better he was!

That, of course, was too much. Jenny, who had once played tennis for her school, planted a firm forehand drive in his eye and then caught hold of his ears and tugged upwards as crisply as she had tugged at the window sash.

Alvin, with a horrid shriek, not only let her go, but threw her forcibly off his lap, nearly losing both ears in the process. Jenny, landing on her knees, had winced, got to her feet, dusted herself down and proceeded to continue opening the window. When it was a foot wide, she turned to him.

'Is that wide enough, Mr Preedy?' she asked affably.

Alvin stared from the window to Jenny's enquiring face and then began to giggle.

'Cor, you take the biscuit!' he announced hoarsely. 'You're pretty cool!'

His laughter was infectious. Jenny smiled too.

'Too true. And if you want to be cool as well, don't try that again.'

Alvin had not tried it again but they had become good friends. The young man she had thought brainless, conceited and selfish turned out to be very shy, quite intelligent and with a genuine gift for music. Once he had admitted he thought her 'posh' and had wanted to see if he could make her seem more human so that he was no longer in awe of her, the air was clear between them and Jenny saw the charm and good sense which she had once thought him incapable of feeling.

She had also penetrated Miss Stott's self-centred and rather whining attitude to life and had discovered that the fat little lady, who had suffered the pain of an arthritic hip stoically for many years, had one absorbing interest in life—her dog, Baby. He was not allowed to visit her in hospital and he was the great love of her life; she would willingly have died to save Baby a moment's pain, Jenny was sure of it. And when Jenny, a dog-lover herself, promised to fetch the dog up one quiet afternoon when the consultants had done their rounds, her gratitude was touching.

'Next week we'll arrange for your brother-in-law to bring him round to the back entrance and I'll smuggle him up to you for an hour,' she promised the old lady. 'After all, other people have children as visitors and I'm sure your little dog will be far less trouble than some of the rather spoilt kids who shriek and rampage round the ward on a Saturday afternoon.'

Even Miss Franklyn's fierceness had become understandable. An active and wiry seventy-four, the sudden, crippling pain in her back had cut short her social life, taken her sleep and generally soured her. Now that she was in hospital and well on the way, she hoped, to being cured, she, too, showed the occasional softer side. Jenny got her books from the library and talked to her about her work, and Miss Franklyn took to calling her 'dear' and submitted to the four-hourly pressure care treatment and the annoyances of her pelvic corset with far less animosity than she had shown at first.

But at last Friday came and it was Jenny's weekend off. To her dismay, Mr Sterne had not forgotten his offer of a lift and so took for granted her acceptance that she had not dared invent an excuse. Instead, she agreed meekly to be outside the hospital gates at five o'clock with her case so that they might drive down to Bath together.

'You get offered a ride in Gerard Sterne's lovely car, he's the hospital's most eligible bachelor, and all you do is moan!' Sister Fox said, smiling. 'I can name you a dozen nurses who'd give their eye-teeth for Mr Sterne to notice them, let alone take them for a drive, and that includes that glamorous secretary of his, from what I've heard. Stan saw her the other day and he said her legs must start at her elbows, yet it's little Nurse Speed who gets the lift!'

'I couldn't care less where his secretary's legs start—or finish for that matter,' Jenny said gloomily. 'I scarcely know Mr Sterne, and what's more, I don't want to! He's probably very nice but I'm not in his league and I don't want to be. And what's more, he offered me the lift because we both live in Bath out of kindness, I suppose, and it'll be purgatory for us both.'

'I know what you mean, but you'll fall for him in the first half-hour, like everyone else does. Just be thankful he's taken a liking to you, because after your bad start it would have been just as easy for him to do the other thing—and that really can make life difficult.'

'I know, but I've never gone out with the medical staff for that reason. Not that I'm going out with Mr Sterne, because I'm not, but . . . oh, well!'

'Why don't you go out with the medical staff?' Sister asked curiously. 'I'm married to one, don't forget. Stan's Mr Rodway's senior houseman on ENT.'

'Well then, you should know better than most that though it's fine if you're right for each other, there's an awful lot of hearts broken whilst you're trying to find out. And it always seems the same way round. Some nice little nurse falls for a doctor after he's taken her out a few times. Then he changes his mind, starts dating another nurse, and the first one becomes miserable and uncertain, stops doing her fair share of the work and hangs around snivelling. So the solution is never to go out with the medical staff and you'll never fall in love and start the ball rolling. See?'

'Not really,' Sister said. 'I thought all nurses wanted to marry doctors. After all, they make pretty good husbands!'

'I don't want a *good* husband, I want a rich, exciting one,' Jenny said scornfully. 'Anyway, I suppose accepting a lift from a consultant isn't like getting into bed with one; now *that* I do draw the line at!'

Sister Fox blinked. 'That's very sensible. Are you referring to drawing the line at consultants, or getting into bed generally?'

'Both. I really don't want to get involved,' Jenny explained. 'I want to have a good time and a career and make some money, and then marry at twenty-five and not a moment sooner. And when I do, I don't intend to work because I'm going to marry someone very rich, so I want to work hard now. Is that so wrong?'

'No. A bit cold-blooded, perhaps, but not wrong. You go off now, Jenny, and have a really good, restful weekend.'

Sister Fox watched her staff nurse leave the building, and then turned her footsteps towards the bus stop which would take her the short ride to her own new little home. She was a lovely girl, Jenny Speed, she reflected, and with looks and character on her side, she probably would marry just when and who she wished. And who was to say that she was wrong to steer clear of the medical staff when it came to dating?

Sandra Fox, with a year's marriage behind her and the first faint stirrings of doubt beginning to plague her, wondered if she herself had been as wise as she thought at the time, to agree to marry Stan before he had even completed his exams. They had been finding things difficult, lately.

She turned right at the gate and saw, out of the corner of her eye, the gleaming silver sports car with its long bonnet draw up beside the kerb. She smiled to herself. At least Jenny would get pleasure out of that marvellous car, no matter how dry she found Mr Sterne!

'Here we are, Nurse, right on time. Jump in!'

Jenny shot a quick, admiring glance at the car and then obeyed Mr Sterne's injunction, putting her small suitcase down on the back seat.

'Thank you,' she said, putting the safety belt on. 'I say, this is a smashing car, sir! I'd like one myself, now I've got a settled job.'

'Would you? Where would you garage it, though? And can you drive?' He glanced swiftly sideways at her, taking in the frivolity of her pink and white sundress and the fact that her hair, usually neatly coiled on top of her head, fell in silky profusion on to bare shoulders. 'You'd better learn to drive first.'

'I can't drive, but I bet there isn't much to it,' Jenny said airily. 'I thought I'd get the car first and then pay someone to give me lessons in it, sort of killing two birds with one stone.'

'And maybe more than birds! Still, saving up for a car on your salary will be a lengthy business, so I dare say pedestrians are safe enough for the present.'

Jenny smiled and smoothed down her skirt. She did not intend to tell him about the modelling jobs, the work in the change booth and all the other small means for a girl of talent and energy to supplement her income when she lived in London!

'Well, it may be a while yet. Do you live in the city, Mr Sterne? If not, do drop me on the outskirts and I'll catch a bus in.'

'It's all right, my home's on the far side of Bath,' Mr Sterne said. 'So I can drop you right outside your door, if you just give me directions.'

'Well, thank you very much,' Jenny said, cursing providence. He had been kind and good company, but she would still rather be on the train! They talked desultorily for the next thirty minutes and when, a few moments later, the silver sports model was drawn off the road and on to a pub car park, Jenny scarcely felt surprised. They were getting on and had quite a lot in common, so if he suggested having a drink here, no doubt it would be a pleasant enough experience.

The consultant got out of the car, came round to the passenger door, opened it, and held out a hand.

'I'm starving and I expect you're hungry, too. Care to join me in a snack and a cool drink? This place is good, I've stopped here before.'

As Jenny nodded and began to scramble out of the car he put cool fingers beneath her elbow and, with his touch, she became aware of a tingling sensation which spread from her fingertips right up to her shoulders and then lurched into her stomach. It was a genuine physical attraction which widened her eyes with astonishment for Jenny, who had been pursued and courted by more than her fair share of men, had never known a feeling quite so intense. She looked up at him, wondering whether he too had shared that dazzling moment, but

there was no way of telling. He looked calm enough—
she just hoped she looked the same!

'All right? Come along, then.'

He led her into the saloon bar, a pleasant, chintzy
place with low, smoke-darkened beams and lots of brass
ornaments. It was empty save for a couple in the corner
and the barman himself. Mr Sterne picked up the menu
which stood on the bar and held it so that she could
read it as he did.

'I can recommend the hot shrimps in butter, if you
like seafood. They come with a substantial salad and
French bread. Or the pâté's a good one—home-made.'

They both decided on the shrimps, accompanied by
a ginger beer each since Mr Sterne said he never drank
alcohol when he was driving. Then, armed with their
drinks and with the barman carrying the tray with their
food on it, they sat down at a table in one of the
windows. It overlooked the back of the inn, which
had an orchard and a duck-pond, and Jenny glanced
appreciatively at the view as she began to eat. The
shrimps were delicious and the salad crisp and good and
she felt rather cossetted and fortunate, with the evening
sunlight pouring in through the window and the room
quiet save for music playing, very softly, in some other
room.

'This is extremely pleasant,' Mr Sterne said, leaning
back in his chair. Dark eyes scanned Jenny lazily. 'Do
you know, the sun on your hair turns it to liquid gold.'

'You've never seen liquid gold,' Jenny said practically, though with a thumping heart. 'Be more practical, Mr Sterne. Say it looks like liquid butter—I dare
say you've seen plenty of that.'

A pair of dark eyebrows rose and his mouth
quirked.

'That, my dear girl, was poetic licence. Don't spoil it by mundane remarks.'

'Oh, poetic licence! I thought it was what we in the nursing profession call soft soap.'

'As it happens, it was no more than the truth. And that's a pretty dress, too.' He picked up his drink and sipped, then saluted her with the glass, his eyes steady on hers across the rim. 'I drink a toast to your bright eyes, Nurse Speed. What are you doing tomorrow night?'

Jenny was so surprised that she nearly choked over a mouthful of shrimp. When she had recovered she eyed her companion severely.

'Nothing. Mr Sterne, surely you're not trying to date me? Is this a consultantly pick-up?'

He sketched a frown, but she thought he was more amused than angry.

'Yes, to both questions. I really see no reason why I shouldn't ask a colleague who happens to live near me to spend a few hours in my company. Now, is that a pick-up?'

'No, not really. But I don't think it would be right for me to go out with you, and I dread to think what Sister Fox would say.'

'Hang what anyone else says! And anyway, Sister's a woman of the world, she'd just tell us to enjoy ourselves. Do you know, you look even more enchanting when you blush than when you don't? Come on, Nurse, come dancing with me tomorrow evening. We'll go to the Assembly Rooms and you can pretend you're a Regency belle!'

'No thank you,' Jenny said demurely, between mouthfuls of French bread. 'I've made it a rule never to go out with a member of the medical staff.'

'So have I,' the surgeon said agreeably, looking as

though butter would not melt in his mouth. 'By and large, I think we're right and one shouldn't mix business with pleasure. But in this instance we're neither of us medical staff. I'm Gerard Sterne, bachelor of the Parish of Bath and you're Jennifer Speed, spinster of same. Why shouldn't we enjoy each other's company? I haven't lived in Bath on a permanent basis for years and I know very few people down here. So why not come dancing?'

'Because it would make our after-life more difficult,' Jenny said, choosing her words rather carelessly. 'You must know it would!'

He raised a brow. He was smiling rather wickedly.

'Speaking for myself, I don't intend to die for love, or not just yet, though I dare say that wasn't quite what you meant! Look, we're both adults and it's quite easy to keep one's life compartmented—I do it all the time. Come out with me while we're in Bath and I promise I won't let the fact that we're friends compromise my hospital formality one jot.'

'I really don't think I should, thank you very much,' Jenny said desperately. 'It's my strongest rule, or nearly my strongest. I don't date doctors or patients or students or anyone at work, and I believe that not going out with colleagues has been my salvation, honestly. You must have noticed how difficult it makes lives on the ward when a nurse is in love with one of the medical staff. I never even go to hospital dances unless I take a partner with me!'

'You really won't come?' Mr Sterne sighed and bit into a piece of French bread. 'How about a picnic on Sunday then, down by the Avon, on my boat? It's a sailing cruiser but it's got an engine so we could glide over the water, swim if you think it's warm enough, lie on the banks and eat our food, drink some wine . . . I'll even buy caviar if it'll tempt you!' He watched her shake her head. 'No? Oh, well!'

And with those words he leaned over the table, took her face between his hands, and plonked a kiss on her mouth, letting his lips linger on hers in what she afterwards decided was a thoroughly immoral and black-mailish manner. She gasped, put up her hands to drag his away, and then, just for a second, surrendered to madness. Then he released her and sat back in his own chair, his eyes gleaming at her beneath lowered lids.

'Well? Surely you aren't going to say no again, and force me to kiss you twice in a public bar?'

'Well, Jenny? Have you enjoyed today?'

It was quite early on Sunday evening, but it was dusky beneath the willow trees that lined the bank of the Avon. The boat was pulled up and tied to a tree stump beneath their secret shade and Gerard Sterne lay back on the cushioned seat, his legs stretched out in front of him. His arm was flung casually round Jenny's shoulders and she was totally relaxed with her head resting against his chest, enjoying his nearness.

Presently, when she nodded, he moved her away from him and she felt the coolness of his lips nuzzling the soft skin at the side of her neck, beneath the fall of her shining hair.

'I've enjoyed it too. I can't get over how good it's been. Quite the best time I've spent in my boat, and out of it. I enjoy my work, but I find myself not wanting to think about tomorrow and the wards and the theatres and the patients.'

Jenny glanced up at his face, dark in the shadows of the willow trees.

'Yes, I love my work too, but I quite understand how you feel.'

He bent his head and his lips began to travel up her throat towards the softness of the flesh beneath her jawline, then across her cheek in little, soft kisses, so that when he took her mouth she was as eager for his kiss as, earlier, she had been shy of such a thing from a consultant. Indeed, in his arms, she thought for a fleeting moment that for two pins . . .

Fortunately, however, experience made her draw back before his caresses became too intimate. They had had a marvellous time but that did not change the fact that he was a surgeon and she a very recently appointed staff nurse. They were poles apart, in fact.

'No further, Jen?'

He had insisted that they use first names, at least whilst they were in Bath, where people would think it very strange to see a couple addressing each other as Mr Sterne and Miss Speed, but Jenny still avoided actually saying Gerard; it sounded so forward!

'No further. Sorry.'

He laughed softly against the smooth skin of her neck.

'Don't apologise. It'll be something to challenge me—to gradually persuade you to lower those formidable defences.'

Jenny laughed too, but sat up and pulled herself gently away from him. Her heart was beating rather too fast for comfort and her breathing was fast too, though she was pleased with her matter-of-fact response.

'I wouldn't count on it. I'm not going to get married for at least four years, so I'm always sensible about this sort of thing.'

'Lovemaking, you mean? But surely you aren't going to keep men at arm's length for four years? I would very much like to see you more often, take you out when we're in town. And I really don't see why we shouldn't have a good time together; we've got on excellently this weekend, have we not?'

Jenny sighed, but let him put his arm round her again.

'Yes, we have and I'd love to go out with you again, so long as you can remember that I'm one of those infuriatingly old-fashioned girls who really don't believe in casual affairs. I'm saving myself, dear sir, for marriage.'

'And why not?' He sounded cheerful. 'Well, in that case we'd better chug back to my boathouse and put this baby to bed before we start back to London.' He yawned, then stood up, making the boat rock wildly, and walked to the bows. 'Hey ho, another weekend nearly over. Want to have a go at driving?'

Jenny moved up to sit beside him, though she refused his offer to let her steer, and the boat slid out of the concealing shadows and into the clear, yellowy-gold light of the setting sun. In the brightness, the two smiled at one another.

What do my old rules matter, Jenny found herself thinking. Damn rules, he's far too nice to lose just because he happens to be a surgeon and therefore a member of the medical profession. I'll let things take their course for a while, anyway.

'Well, how did the weekend go? How's Mrs Speed?'

'She's fine, thanks, and full of glee that I'm a staff nurse at last.'

Katrina and Jenny were in the canteen with their heads together over a macaroni cheese and a plateful of spaghetti bolognese. It was the first time they had

had a chance to talk, since Katrina was on a late and Jenny on an early, but Jenny was longing to talk about her weekend.

'Go anywhere exciting in Bath? Meet any old beaux?'

'No. Well, I spent Sunday on the river with Mr Sterne.' Jenny watched Katrina's mouth drop open with considerable satisfaction. 'Nothing serious, of course, but we had a picnic and chugged up the river in his cruiser, and then dined at a little place he knew. It was great fun. He's good company, not a bit *stern*, ho ho, like he is at work.'

Katrina spooned up macaroni cheese and spoke thickly through a mouthful, her eyes twinkling.

'So your firmest rule is broken at last! Thou shalt not go out with the medical staff is no more, I assume?'

'Oh, you can't count a consultant, surely? I mean, how could I refuse? It would have seemed awfully churlish, and he's a lot older than me.'

Katrina nearly choked over her macaroni cheese, then pointed an accusing fork at her friend

'Oh fie on you, Jennifer Speed! You wouldn't have the slightest compunction in saying a very firm no, if that was how you felt. And as for his being old—gosh, he can't be more than thirty-two or three, and he's a dishy devil. He must have been, to make you break rule number one. Tell me, how did he do it?'

'He kissed me. Right in the middle of a public bar, and rather too forcibly for true politeness. But cripes, he can kiss! Instead of remembering to aim a blow for women's lib, I have to admit I enjoyed it, and when he said if I kept repeating my refusal he'd be forced to kiss me again, I gave in gracefully.'

'I bet you did! He's a fast worker though. Rumour has it that he likes women, so don't you go falling for him! Rumour also has it that the glamorous secretary is more than an employee.'

'I wouldn't be such a fool—how can I, when I don't want to get married for another four years?' Jenny finished her spaghetti and stood up. 'Want a coffee? I'll go and get two if you like and then I must fly because Mr Sterne's operating tomorrow so he'll be round later.'

'I dare say it will be the first time you've seen him since Sunday?' At Jenny's nod, Katrina grinned. 'Just remember not to go giving any games away. Don't go calling him Gerard!'

'As if I would! See you later, Kat!'

Jenny did wonder how she would manage to retain a straight face if Gerard should smile at her knowingly, but in the event it was easier than she expected, partly because when he did come he was late and in a hurry, and partly because both of them were determined to maintain formal relations in hospital hours. Jenny joined the surgical team for the round when Sister rang for her, stealing a quick glance at Mr Sterne's profile as they made their way up the corridor. He was very good-looking, probably the handsomest man she had ever dated, and it also struck her that at thirty-one, he was also the oldest. She realised that in the world of modelling and magazines, where most of her male acquaintances lay, the men were, on the whole, in their middle twenties. So perhaps it is his sheer worldly experience which knocks me off my feet, she told herself, as the team entered the first room.

What was more, all his patients seemed to be doing well. Mrs Franklyn said that the pain seemed a little easier. Miss Stott, with her hip replacement operation successfully performed the previous Thursday, was able to move around the bed, although Mr Sterne insisted on an abduction block so that she did not inadvertently cross her legs. The only person awaiting surgery who had been in a while was Bob Anderson, and this was only because a severe head cold had forced Mr Sterne to put off the operation for a week.

After the round, Sister bore Mr Sterne off to her office and Jenny went back to Room Four, since she had promised to test Bob—they were now on first-name terms—with a list of prepared questions on his text.

'I forgot to ask the old man whereabouts on the list I am tomorrow,' Bob said as soon as she slipped into the room. 'Could you possibly find out for me, Jenny? My sister says she'll visit if I'm early, but won't bother if I'm late, because she thinks I might still be dopey.'

'I'll go down as soon as Mr Sterne's out of there and let you know,' Jenny said readily. 'The only reason patients aren't always told is that some worry if they know. But you won't, will you?'

'Course not. Worry more not knowing. Off you pop then, sweetheart, and don't forget to come back and test me!'

The surgeon was walking briskly across the end hall as Jenny left Bob's room, so she was able to go straight into the office. Sister sat behind the desk, a hand on her brow, looking tired and unhappy, but she conjured up a smile for Jenny's sake and tried to straighten her drooping back.

'Can I help you, Jenny?'

'Can I help *you*?' countered Jenny, very much concerned. 'You look awful, Sandra. Is anything the matter?' Sister Fox had told her that they usually used first names when alone, and she had soon grown friendly with the older girl.

'It's just that Stan and I had a bit of a row at lunch-time. Nothing serious, but it has occurred to me that we row rather often, these days. Sometimes I hardly seem to open my mouth without him snarling at me, and today I made some totally innocuous remark about Mrs Franklyn's back, and he almost shouted at me for "talking shop". Yet I know he's under considerable strain, with his finals coming up soon. I was a fool to answer back. I should have just smoothed him down, or agreed with him, instead of saying he was being petty.'

'I'm sorry, I wish I could help. Why do you row, as a rule? Is it anything specific or just over how many angels can dance on the point of a needle?'

The older girl laughed and began to look more cheerful.

'It's funny you should say that, because when he's tired and strained he seems to want to argue, and angels on a needle-point are just about the average standard of the fights he wants to pick! But the really absurd thing is that we married because our interests were similar, really we did, yet all of a sudden he says he's tired of what he calls my "ward talk". Says it gets on his nerves to have arthoplasty and bone grafts and stomach pumps and the psychiatric treatment of over-dose patients shoved down his throat at meal-times. But I don't! Or I try not to! Only I can almost feel him waiting for me to forget and put my foot in it, mention a patient, so that he can snarl. Awful, isn't it?'

'Yes, it is, and very unfair,' Jenny said. 'I bet he does the same in reverse, only you're too nice to mention it. I bet you have tonsils for breakfast and adenoids for tea!'

'We used to, only all of a sudden he stopped talking about his work and the people on ENT.' Sandra stood up, pushing her hair back under her cap. 'Sorry, love. I've got to learn to put up with it until after his finals, I suppose. What did you come in for, Jen? I'm sure it wasn't to listen to my troubles.'

'It was to see the list, actually, so that I can tell Bob Anderson whether he's early or late tomorrow. His sister says she'll visit if he's early, so he wants to tell her yes or no.'

'I see. Well, you tell him to warn his sister off tomorrow, though he's first, as it happens. Have you never nursed a bone graft before?'

'No, I haven't. There are a good many things I haven't nursed before.'

'Yes, of course. Well, I wouldn't advise visitors on the day of the operation itself. He'll feel pretty rotten one way and another. Tell him to put her off until Wednesday, if he can.'

Making her way down the corridor again, Jenny found herself thinking that Sandra's marital troubles only served to confirm her own conviction that there was no sense in getting involved with anyone who worked in the same hospital as oneself. Poor girl, scarcely married twelve months and finding herself continually put in the wrong!

It occurred to Jenny, too, that Stan's behaviour might well have a cause other than his finals and tiredness. One of her flatmates, Mandy Crewe, worked on ENT and would confirm willingly enough whether there was any reason why Dr Stanley Fox was suddenly difficult to live with.

In the meantime, however, there was Bob. It was all very well to tell him to put his sister off, but Jenny had no desire to worry her patient by telling him that he would not feel up to visitors next day. Tough though he was, she knew that Bob *did* worry about the operation. He would have been very thick-skinned had he not done so. She decided that she would generalise a bit, and went into his room, telling him briefly that visitors were not encouraged on ops-day and that his sister would be well-advised to change her trip to London to the Wednesday.

Bob pulled a face, though he was very pleased that he was to be first down in the morning.

'Right, I'll ring Marjorie tonight and tell her to leave it until Wednesday. Are you on an early or late tomorrow, Jen?'

'Early. Seven-thirty until four. Why?'

'Well, couldn't you visit me? I hate it when seven o'clock comes and people keep walking up and down the corridor and no one comes through my door.'

'Well, I might stretch a point and pop back in,' Jenny conceded. 'I might even dress up in my best for you—I adore wearing pretty summer dresses!'

After that she went along to Mrs Franklyn's room to rub cream into that lady's pressure points and to ask if she would like afternoon tea. Other patients, Mrs Franklyn had inferred, might loll about decadently drinking tea and eating cucumber sandwiches in the middle of the afternoon, but she was made of sterner stuff. That had been her attitude last week, but Jenny had detected a softening since then. The sheer boredom of being on pelvic traction had been beginning to tell, so she decided to have another go, and was duly rewarded. Mrs Franklyn graciously consented to take tea and sandwiches, but when Jenny suggested that she might turn on the television set she became the recipient of a very repellent look!

'I am not yet so desperate that I would watch television before the six o'clock news,' she said firmly.

And then, relenting, she added that, if Jenny wished, she might take a message through to Miss Stott's room. The two elderly ladies, though now both tied by the leg, so to speak, continued to keep up their unlikely friendship through the medium of small notes, the odd telephone call and constant messages passed by the nursing staff. The previous week, Jenny had had the felicity of seeing Mr Sterne pressed into service, and had muffled her mirth along with the rest of the team as he fought to convince his old teacher that she could not make him her errand boy.

'Yes, I want to see Miss Stott presently,' Jenny admitted. 'What must I tell her?'

'Just that I'm taking tea today, which is a sign of *extreme* boredom, and that I am told charcoal biscuits sweeten the breath wonderfully.' At Jenny's raised brows she added a rider to this strange remark. 'It's Baby, Nurse. He suffers from bad breath, Miss Stott tells me. She says it is positively the only thing that stops her from allowing him on her bed at night.' Mrs Franklyn, no believer in laxness towards dogs or humans, frowned. 'Perhaps it might be as well not to pass that message on, now that I consider. I should not like to be the cause of Miss Stott allowing that animal any more liberties.'

Jenny bit back a question about Baby's liberties and assured Mrs Franklyn that it would be a kindness to tell Miss Stott about the charcoal biscuits. Then, armed with Mrs Franklyn's order for afternoon tea and the message, she set off up the corridor.

Miss Stott was jubilant because Mr Sterne had promised her that, in a day or so, she might get up from her bed, move about a little, and perhaps even get wheeled in a chair to see her friend next door.

'So now, Nurse, all that I need to make me *quite* well is that time you promised me with Baby.' Her anxious eyes swivelled round at Jenny. 'You did mean it, didn't you? You can't imagine how I miss him!'

'I can, actually,' Jenny said. 'Look, how would Thursday afternoon do, at about four? The visitors will have gone from the ordinary wards and the consultants will have done their rounds and everyone else will be busy with tea. I don't suppose I'm breaking any rules, because visiting on the private ward has always been much less hidebound than on the other ones, but I'll meet your brother-in-law by the back entrance nevertheless. I've okayed it with Sister Fox,' she added truthfully. 'Oh, and before I forget, I've a message from Mrs Franklyn.'

When she had discharged her errand, Jenny went along to the small kitchen where the staff prepared their own tea and coffee and sometimes did invalid cooking for a patient. When she reached it, Pat Roach and Dr Mongresin were comfortably ensconced at opposite ends of the kitchen table, watching the progress of two kettles, which were on the top of the cooker and just beginning to simmer. Pat smiled, but Pierre Mongresin got to his feet, waved a hand, and then patted the table.

'Come and sit down, Nurse! Pat and I have just been discussing my colleague on Orthopaedics. We're pulling him to pieces.'

'Who, Nat Phillips—Dr Phillips, I should say?' Mr Sterne's registrar was young, tall and baby-faced, with straw-coloured hair. He was very shy and had scarcely spoken more than two or three words to Jenny, but she rather liked him. 'He's nice. Why should you pull him to pieces?'

Pierre smiled.

'Nat's harmless, I don't know about nice. No, we

were discussing Gerard Sterne. Not a man I care for.'

Pierre Mongresin was generally much admired by the nursing staff for his thick, black curls, his romantic dark eyes and his very slight French accent. Now Jenny discovered that he had never appealed to her much. His eyes were not romantically dark but sly, and his accent almost certainly false. She frowned at him.

'Really? I shouldn't imagine you're in much of a position to hold an opinion, Dr Mongresin.'

The Anglo-Frenchman was not used to having his views waved aside by mere staff nurses. He looked sharply at her, then back to Pat Roach, who had her mouth at half-cock. Plainly, Pat thought that Jenny was being very unwise!

'And why should I not, Nurse? No, I should say Jenny, of course, it's friendlier. Why should I not know about Mr Sterne?'

'Because you're medical and he's surgical. And I would prefer that you did not use my first name,' Jenny snapped. She went over to the dresser and began taking cups and saucers down from the shelves. 'Are there any biscuits, Pat?'

'Yes, there's a box on the top shelf,' Pat said, her voice sounding cooler than it normally did. Goodness, Jenny thought, shooting an apprehensive glance at her junior, let us hope that Pat hasn't fallen for this fellow's doubtful charms—he isn't the sort to waste his beauty on a mere nurse!

'Right. Could you get them out? I'll do a tray for Sister and myself if you and Dr Mongresin want to shred characters in here.'

'Really, Jenny, what a fuss! I had no intention of denigrating Mr Sterne's work, which has always been highly regarded by all the medical staff. It's just his behaviour with his secretary that I was questioning.'

Jenny turned round, the tray in her hands, and saw the look that was being turned on her by the young registrar. It was an extremely knowing yet speculative look. The look of one who is thinking, *there is more to this sudden defence of Mr Sterne than meets the eye. The question is, what?*

Heavens, what an idiot she had been! It would be all round the hospital that she fancied Gerard like crazy if she did not take care. Quickly, she put the tray on the table and smiled blindingly at Dr Mongresin.

'Oh, you mean social gossip! Goodness, you must have thought I was being terribly high-minded, but he's an excellent surgeon. I'm nursing his cases, and I really do disapprove of medical men cutting each other up behind their backs. Which some do—but not you, Pierre!'

She wondered whether her use of his first name would be frowned on; whether she had, in fact, overdone the sudden capitulation. But one glance at his complacent expression assured her that she had not. Pat, on the other hand, looked rather wary. Now why would that be?

Of course, Pat probably rather fancied him, for all she was a respectably engaged girl! Jenny, relieved that Pat had not questioned her attack on Pierre and then her sudden change of face, perched herself on the table between the two of them.

'Well? What is all this about Mr Sterne's secretary? Sister says her legs go up to her elbows, that's about all I know.'

'Aha, but they say down in the medical secretaries' offices that ten days ago Janice Quinton was unbearably pleased with herself, said she'd got Sterne tied up, wild about her, and expected a proposal any day. And since then—nothing. Very polite, very charming, but not in the least amorous. So what has gone wrong? Pat here thinks he's got fed-up with Janice's increasingly proprietorial attitude. She says he's not the type to bleat round in a woman's wake, but I don't think he ever did. I think he's met someone else!'

'What sort of proposal was she expecting?' Jenny said cautiously. 'Not marriage, after a mere . . . Well, it can't have been a long acquaintance.'

'No-oo, she's only been attached to the Orthopaedic team for three weeks. She used to be with Ophthalmic,' Pat said, entering into the discussion with obvious zest. 'She's a good secretary, I believe, but very much a man's woman, and the new ophthalmic registrar's a woman and a very pretty one too. I don't know the truth of it, I just know that they had a blazing row one day and Janice applied for a transfer.'

'I see. What does she look like—this Janice?'

'Well, women say she's a bottle blonde,' Pierre said judiciously. 'At any rate, she's got ash blonde hair. She's tall and I suppose one could say voluptuous, with features a bit like a shop window model or one of those American film extras you see on television—you know, fairly interchangeable. That sounds spiteful, but it describes her rather well. Plastic good looks, only she's got something more.'

'Yes, she has. As they say in romances, she exudes sexuality,' Pat said eagerly. 'Honestly, that girl isn't capable of giving a man a straight glance! It always smoulders with Eastern promise.'

'I must meet her. You never answered the question about what sort of proposal she expected, by the way,' Jenny said, leaving her perch as the first kettle started to boil. Her two companions looked at her with some surprise.

'What sort of proposal would you expect, if you were a sexy secretary and your boss was a consultant? She thought he'd ask her to move in with him, of course.'

'Oh.' Jenny poured boiling water into the first of the teapots. 'Not marriage, then?'

'Marriage?' Pierre snorted. 'Sterne's managed to keep his head clear of the noose for the last thirty odd years, so I can't imagine why he should take the plunge now, and with a little doxy at that! She was old Buckler's bit on the side whilst she worked for Ophthalmic, you know.'

'Well, but they say that about everyone, to one degree or another,' Jenny protested. 'A reasonable-looking consultant is always reckoned to be involved with either the prettiest sister or his secretary, and it's never been true, from what I've heard. It's just that it enlivens people's dull lives to believe ill of others, I suppose.'

'Yes, I know what you mean, but it really was true about Janice and Mr Buckler. He had a flat quite near the hospital which he used on Monday and Wednesday nights, because they're his operating days, and once he was needed urgently at about four in the morning, so one of his side-kicks rushed round to the flat. Apparently they tried the phone and couldn't get him. And this fellow—it was his houseman, actually—this fellow knocked on the door, and guess who opened it, all disarrayed, in a *very* revealing nightie? And said next day that she'd been to a party and missed her last train home and Mr Buckler had offered her a bed for the night?'

'Don't tell me, I can guess! Well, I can't see Mr Sterne taking another man's leavings, can you?'

'Yes,' Dr Mongresin said promptly. 'Why not? She's hot stuff is Janice, and as I said, no one, including Janice, expected him to marry her, just to make a dishonest woman of her!'

'I give up,' Jenny said. She put the cups and a plateful of biscuits out on the tray. 'I'd better take these along to the office. See you later, Pat.'

She hurried along the corridor towards Sister's office, but a most unwelcome thought had just occurred to her and kept drumming through her head. *Jenny and Gerard, those names go nicely together,* he had said idly, when he had first insisted that they use each other's Christian names. Had he just been repeating last week's flirtation? Had he said, last week, *Janice and Gerard, those names go nicely together*?

She reached Sister's office, opened the door with some difficulty, with the tray balanced on her hip, and slid into the room.

'Tea for two, Sandra,' she announced. 'A little break while the patients have their afternoon rest, then it's back to work.'

Working up and down the corridor for the rest of the afternoon, creaming pressure points, adjusting tractions, taking bedpans through with a paper towel over them, picking the full ones up, emptying them and popping them into the steriliser, she wondered many times just exactly how she herself regarded Gerard Sterne. He had been a delightful companion, his lovemaking had been an experience she very much wanted to repeat, and she definitely looked forward to going out with him again. But did she want the friendship to go further? Did she want a more serious relationship between herself and the consultant? It was not easy to answer her question while she was still swayed by remembering the feel of his mouth and hands. And if she was honest, she viewed with considerable dismay the prospect of not seeing him again socially.

But it was possible that he was just passing the time in Bath, she told herself, remaking a bed with clean sheets and putting a fresh chart on the board at the bottom of it. He may simply have wanted someone to amuse him while he was in a city he did not know terribly well. He might just have mentioned taking her out again when they got back to London out of politeness.

But Jenny had been out with too many men to fool herself completely. In her heart, she was sure she had not heard the last of Gerard Sterne!

CHAPTER THREE

TUESDAY morning began with prepping Bob Anderson for his bone graft operation. Despite his tough appearance and talk, it was clear to Jenny that the young man was nervous, though he kept assuring her that he was not and could not wait to get down to the operating theatre and back on the ward. Jenny and Pat gave him his operating gown and then came back to put his bedsocks on for him, which brought a genuine grin to his rather pallid face. Then they took his valuables away in a sealed envelope and Jenny bade him turn his face away whilst she injected him with the premed jab which would not only dry up his saliva but would also ensure that he was already both sleepy and tranquil by the time the theatre staff got their hands on him.

'I'll come with you as far as the ante-room,' Jenny told him. 'Then, of course, the theatre staff take over. But they'll do their usual quick and efficient job and then you'll be opening your eyes again and wondering where you are. And the first thing you'll see will be my face, because Sister said I was to come back here until you were right round.'

Jenny knew that he would be brought round in the recovery room, but so few patients remembered that part of the experience afterwards that she felt her boast was safe enough.

'If I wake up and see your face I'll think I'm in heaven,' Bob said with rather forced gallantry. 'Is it nine o'clock yet? It must be!'

'No, you've got another seven minutes to go,' Jenny said, consulting her fob watch. 'Just you lie there and think of sunshine, green meadows and lambs frolicking in the grass, and the porter will be here before you know it.'

He sighed but lay back obediently on his pillows and presently, when his lids drooped, Jenny left the room, though with the door ajar, and went down to Sister's office. Sandra was there, busily writing up her notes, but she looked up and smiled when Jenny entered.

'They've just rung through; a porter's on his way for our first patient. How is Bob—very nervous? Or is he getting drowsy?'

'Both, I think. If the porter's on his way, shall I walk down to the lifts? He may need a hand manoeuvring the trolley in that confined space.'

'Actually, they get pretty used to doing it themselves. But you can countersign Bob's envelope before I put it in the safe.'

'Pleasure.' Jenny bent over the book and scrawled her signature in the appropriate column, then watched as Sister put the envelope into the small safe behind her desk. 'I know it's necessary to take care of valuables on the other wards, but why do we have to do it up here? Everyone has their own room and we don't get strangers wandering around.'

'Oh, no? What about that newshound or whoever he was who tried to interview Mrs Widdowes last week? And the cleaning staff change quite a lot. And even nurses have been tempted sometimes by the carelessness of private patients in leaving ten years' salary in diamonds hanging on the tap in the bathroom!' She turned to consult the list which hung behind her desk. 'We've only one other patient for theatre this morning and that's the hernia, Mr McRae. He won't go down until noon because he's last on the list, so there's no point in prepping him yet.' Both girls turned as a tap on the door heralded a visitor. 'Oh, good morning, Mr Richards. Nurse will show you where the patient is.'

Mr Richards was a brawny porter in his late fifties, a great favourite with the nursing staff because of his willingness to help and his unvarying good-temper. He greeted them cheerfully, then waved his paper at Sister.

'Where is 'e, then? Robert Anderson, number one, lucky for some! Let's get a move on, gals, we don't want 'is nibs to find 'imself all dressed up with no one to do!'

'He's in Room Six,' Jenny said. 'I'm coming with you to give you a hand with him. He's drowsy already and his leg's pretty bad, so he needs careful handling.'

'Righty ho, Nurse!' Mr Richards followed her along the corridor, his trolley before him, and swung it through as Jenny opened Bob's door wide. 'Morning, Mr Anderson! And 'ow are you this morning?'

Back in his bed, which was elevated at the foot so that his injured leg would be less likely to swell, Bob Anderson slept. Jenny checked that the suction clamp was correctly adjusted on the postovac drain so that there could be no back-flow of air, that the intravenous drip was working smoothly and that the plaster, which was still damp, was showing no signs of leakage, and then sat down by the bed. Bob had already come round once, in the recovery room, and Sister had said he ought to do so again in ten or fifteen minutes, but because there were no fellow-patients to keep an eye on him, as there would have been in the ordinary ward, it was always necessary for a staff member to remain in a patient's room until he or she had completely come out of the fog of the anaesthetic.

It was actually twenty minutes before Bob began to stir again, but this time he came right round, glancing up at her and saying thickly, 'Is it all over? Can I have a drink?'

'Yes, it's over, but you can't have a drink yet, I'm afraid, though you're welcome to a mouth-wash.' Jenny fizzed a tablet in a half-glassful of water and handed it to her patient, taking the precaution, though, of holding the metal kidney bowl herself. 'Rinse it round and then spit. No swallowing allowed. Cheating will probably end in tears, as they say.'

Bob rinsed obediently, spat, then smiled.

'That's so much better! I'm sure my mouth was full of white glue.'

'Yes, it's a horrible feeling. How does the rest of you feel?'

Bob considered for a moment, then answered with great frankness, 'Bloody. Can I go to sleep now, for a bit?'

'It's the best thing you can do, and when you wake up, you'll feel right as rain.' Jenny drew the bell from its resting place until it was actually lying in Bob's palm. 'The bell's in your hand. If you need anything at all, just ring. Now, reassure me that you know what I'm talking about and see if you can press the bell to good effect.'

Bob smiled and feebly pressed the bell. Then, even as Jenny was smiling her approval, she saw him relax in sleep.

'Ah, Nurse, I believe you were with Mr Anderson when he came round. Is everything all right? He's sleeping now, but was he in much pain? I've given Sister an injection for him if he wakes in much discomfort, and I've checked on Mr Crimshaw as well; he seems to be responding nicely.'

Jenny was in the sluice, putting a huge bouquet of flowers into one of the very handsome vases which belonged to the ward. She turned at the sound of the voice, but scarcely needed the confirmation of her eyes to know that it was Mr Sterne. She had been aware, from the very first syllable, who shared the room with her. However, she kept on with her work, tucking the gypsophila fronds decoratively in among the dark red roses even as she answered his questions.

'Mr Anderson was in some pain, sir, though he's asleep now. I checked the drainage from the iliac crest and the suction clamp, which was all satisfactory. The drip was moving nicely and the plaster was clean fifteen minutes ago, when I checked. And Mr Crimshaw is wide awake, though we thought he'd sleep after the pethidine. In fact, I've only just . . .'

Mr Sterne shut the door behind him and crossed the floor in a couple of long strides. He put his hands on her shoulders, pulled her towards him and kissed her lightly on the mouth.

'Well done, Nurse! What an age away Sunday seems—I've missed, you Jenny.'

'Yes, I've . . . but we're at *work*! You said . . .' Jenny began, and was kissed again, with more force. When they moved apart he looked down at her, smiling lazily

'Work? Who's working? The moment I'm alone with you the occasion becomes social. How about dinner tonight?'

'Well, I'm visiting Mr Anderson around seven o'clock so that he isn't solitary when everyone else has someone to see them. Though I don't suppose I'll stay long—he probably won't want me to if he's still drowsy.'

Gerard Sterne's eyebrows rose. 'I'm not sure I should encourage that. You work hard enough without adding evening visits. Look, if you arrive at six-forty instead of seven, and leave earlier too, I can pick you up outside the gates at seven-twenty. Grab a sandwich at the flat when you get back there to tide you over, and we'll go straight to the cinema and then dine afterwards.'

'The cinema? I didn't know consultants took their molls to the cinema!' Jenny's eyes were sparkling. 'What's on?'

'*Gandhi*, actually. I missed it first time round and I've regretted it since. But if you've seen it, we could go somewhere else.'

'No, I haven't, though I meant to. All right then, that would be lovely, I'll come. Oh, and thank you very much.'

'Good. Twenty past seven outside the gates, then.' He pulled her close and the look on his face, which had been strictly practical, blurred into another look as his mouth came down over hers . . . and behind them, the door began to open.

Mr Sterne was half-way back to the door by the time Sister's head appeared round it. He raised an eyebrow at her, for Sister was obviously rather surprised to find a senior consultant in the sluice!

'Yes, Sister?'

'Oh, good afternoon, Mr Sterne. I just wanted to tell Staff that she had better leave the rest of the flowers for Nurse Wellman—Mr McRae's drip needs adjusting again; the flow doesn't want to flow, if you see what I mean.'

'Right. Off with you, Nurse. Go and fiddle with the drip.'

Without so much as another glance in her direction, Mr Sterne left the room and Jenny, hoping that she looked calmer than she felt, approached Sister, the vase of roses held in both hands.

'Right, I might as well deliver these to Mrs Hudson on my way though, since they're ready. I'll do the rest later, if I get time.'

Sister walked with her a short way down the corridor, and Jenny knew that she was dying to ask what Mr Sterne had been doing in the sluice, so she forestalled the question by volunteering the information.

'He's a very caring surgeon, Mr Sterne, isn't he? Apparently you told him that I'd been with Bob when he came round, and he wanted to know whether the patient had been in much pain and how he felt. I was only glad that I was working in the sluice and not dodging out for a smoke!'

Sister laughed. 'But you don't smoke, Jenny!'

Jenny slowed down as she reached Mrs Hudson's door and laughed too.

'No, but I could easily have been doing nothing, you know what it's like. Even the best nurses stop occasionally and just stand and think. But there I was, up to my elbows in roses . . .'

Sister nodded and turned back towards her office.

'Yes, I know what you mean, but you're being a bit harsh on Mr Sterne, I think. He does understand that nurses are only human and need a break occasionally.'

Jenny, going about her business once more, reflected that Sister had certainly got one thing right. Mr Sterne knew very well that *one* nurse was human, and that nurse was looking forward to her evening out very much indeed.

*   *   *

'Where are you off to tonight, Jenny? And why so extra-specially smart? I thought you were between men at the moment.'

Mandy, a petite red-head with slanting green eyes and dimples which appeared whenever she smiled, glanced enviously at Jenny as she came into the kitchen. Jenny's hair was loose and, in a crisp white blouse and her dark blue skirt, with a scarlet silk scarf knotted round her throat and elegant scarlet sandals on her feet, she looked both elegant and patriotic.

'Actually I'm hospital visiting, but I'm glad you like the red, white and blue look. I wondered if I was overdoing it, especially since I'm going on afterwards to see *Gandhi*.' Jenny went into the pantry and looked consideringly at the array of tins on the shelves. 'What are you having on that toast? Can I share it if I open the tins?'

'Yes, of course. I thought beans.' Mandy began to put the slices of bread under the grill. 'Who are you visiting? Helen and I are going to a photographic exhibition since Helen's off tonight.'

'Well, I haven't found myself a millionaire yet, but this chap's a student vet and very nice. Do we have any brown sauce? I adore it on beans.'

'There's some on the bottom shelf I think,' Mandy said. 'A vet, eh? But I thought you said you'd never go out with a member of the medical profession? And it's no use you shaking your head at me because a vet is a doctor, albeit only of animals. Or doesn't a vet's wife suffer the same hardships as a doctor's wife does? I heard you, going on at Katrina the other night, moaning about the anti-social hours and the fact that young doctors can be on call for some ridiculously long time, like forty-six hours out of forty-eight. Isn't a vet medical?'

'Yes, but I'm interested in Bob as a case, not as a suitor,' Jenny pointed out virtuously. 'In fact, Mandy, I'm one of the few women I know who doesn't let her mind slide from a first kiss to marriage—and bed, of course—within two minutes of meeting a fellow.'

'It isn't only minds that slide from kisses to bed, these days,' Mandy observed gloomily, turning the thick slices of bread. 'I've been having a nice, friendly relationship with the new houseman on ENT and blow me down if he didn't take me to the flicks, two nights ago. Afterwards he bought us both fish and chips and invited me back to his flat, and once there, calmly announced that we'd eat and then "get it together". Of course when I said no, I didn't want that sort of relationship, he tried to pretend that I was the only girl in the world who wasn't panting to jump into bed with him, and more or less said I ought to see a doctor about my unnatural lack of urges. With a lot of men, it's bed or you're a spoilsport the first time he decides he fancies you. I don't know why all these women's libbers think the Pill liberated them. It simply makes you seem mean to deny the most casual acquaintance enormous liberties!'

Jenny laughed and tipped the beans into a pan, then transferred it to the top of the cooker.

'Yes, I've noticed. But I dare say that if you asked your mother—no, perhaps not your mother, but someone of her generation—she would tell you that in *her* day, men just said not to be afraid of unwanted babies, *they'd* take care of all that.'

'And didn't, in most cases, judging by what I've heard.'

'True. Tea or coffee, Mandy?'

'Coffee, please. And then I'd better go and change.

Not that going to a photographic exhibtion is a high-fashion occasion.'

'No, but you'll want to wear something cool, it's a warm evening.' Jenny slid on to a chair and pulled it close to the table. She put brown sauce over her beans and then took her first mouthful. 'Mm, I do adore baked beans! Mandy, I've kept meaning to ask you, you work with Dr Fox, don't you?'

'That's right. He's a nice chap, though he's up to his eyes in studying for his finals, or ought to be. Why?'

'What's the current gossip doing the rounds about him at the moment?'

Mandy laughed and sat herself down opposite Jenny.

'I suppose you mean the ophthalmic registrar. Yes, there's no doubt that Foxie's rather smitten, but that doesn't mean that Dr Moran's going to do more than play up to him—she's got more nous, I should think. He's married.'

'Ah, but you think . . . well, would you say he was keen? Making a play for this woman?'

'Yes, he jolly well is. Perhaps he's only so ardent because the competition's pretty stiff; you know how men can be, and she's remarkably attractive. And, though I like her, she does play up to all the men. Someone said only the other day, actually, that it was a pity she didn't steer clear of Foxie, with his finals coming up, because it looked as though his infatuation would mean he wouldn't work anywhere near hard enough. But he's got a bit of time yet. Perhaps he'll realise she's trifling with his affections and pull himself together.'

'Hmm, that's bad. So he's got his eye on ophthalmics! That would account for a lot.' Jenny took a huge mouthful of beans on toast and spoke thickly through it. 'He's married to the sister on my ward, you see. She's a bit edgy, though I'm sure she doesn't know why.'

'Lor, yes! I remember you calling her Sister Fox, now you mention it. Pretty, is she?'

Jenny finished her food and pushed back her chair.

'Yes, very pretty. She's got short, dark hair done in one of those sleek, head-fitting styles, and very nice dark eyes—quite a good figure, too. And she's intelligent. But I suppose beside an ophthalmic registrar . . '

'Yes, Dr Moran's clever, all right, and stunning too. What are you going to do about it? It might be better to warn her, you know, though I dare say you'll feel it's none of your business. But if it were me, I think I'd rather know. Then at least she can fight back.'

'I'll think it over and let you know what I decide. And now I'm off for the Annabel Goodson ward. I trust they treat visitors with respect and don't expect them to soil their hands!'

'I say, you look super, Jenny!'

Jenny pulled up a chair beside Bob Anderson's bed and smiled at him.

'You noticed my finery! That means you're feeling better than you felt earlier. Did you eat something at supper time?'

He nodded. He was propped up on his pillows now but he looked rumpled and weary, though his eyes showed that no trace of the anaesthetic lingered as they scanned Jenny's appearance.

'Good. Has your sister come or will she be along tomorrow?'

'She'll be here tomorrow. Better, really, since I'm still not making dazzling conversation I'm afraid.' He hesitated, then spoke gruffly, not meeting her gaze. 'My hip—I hadn't expected it to be so bloody sore. I'm used to my leg hurting, of course.'

'Yes, Mr Sterne said it was a nasty business for the first day or two. Poor old Bob. Feeling drowsy, are you? That'll be the pain-killing injection.'

'Pain-killing injection?' Bob looked puzzled. 'But I haven't had any injection—not since the op. And I've been lying here worrying because I know I shan't sleep with the pain nagging me.'

Jenny sighed and got to her feet.

'Leave this place for a couple of hours and the organisation goes to pot! Hang on a second, Bob, while your visitor turns herself back into Nurse Speed, and you shall have that injection in two ticks.'

She went down to Sister's office and found Sister Lucas, the night sister, sitting behind the desk. She smiled at her visitor with more politeness than a fellow member of staff warranted before recognising Jenny, and then she laughed.

'Good lord, Staff, you *are* posh. I thought you were a visitor! Can I help you?'

'Oh, please, Sister Lucas, may I look in the drug book? Mr Sterne was in earlier and he told me he'd left permission for Mr Anderson to have a pain-killing injection as soon as he woke and I thought Sister Fox would have passed the message on.'

Sister Lucas reached the drug book down from the shelf and turned the pages, then tutted.

'Yes, it's here, but Sandra didn't say anything. I'll come along with you now, though it'll make him sleepy again, I'm afraid. Perhaps he'd rather leave it until your visit is over?'

She was smiling, but Jenny shook her head. 'No, I'm sure not, the poor lad really is in pain. He doesn't mind nodding off in front of me. He'll do it quite often in the next few days. Can I help you—get the trolley, anything like that?'

'No, it's all right thank you, Staff, I'll just pop along with the syringe and it'll be done in a jiffy.' The sister went to the drugs cupboard and to her trolley, laid up ready for the evening round, and then, armed with the necessary equipment, set off beside Jenny back to Room Six.

With the injection making itself felt, Bob lay back and smiled drowsily at Jenny and Sister briskly left the room, closing the door softly behind her.

'Tell me why you're all dressed up, I can't kid myself that it was for me,' Bob asked.

'Well, not just for you,' Jenny conceded. 'I'm going out to see *Gandhi* afterwards—the film, you know—and then to dinner.'

'Super. Who's your boyfriend?'

Jenny smiled. She had no intention of telling Bob or anyone apart from Katrina who she was going out with!

'What makes you think you'd be any the wiser if I told you?'

He yawned. 'I suppose I took it for granted that a nurse as beautiful as you would have bagged herself a doctor.' He yawned again. 'Have a lovely time and come and tell Uncle Bob all about it in the morning.'

'That's a very gracious dismissal.' Jenny got to her feet and rumpled his hair. 'I hope you have a good night, Bob, but if you don't, just you ring for Sister Lucas—she'll see you're all right.'

'I will. Have I ever told you I love you, Nurse?' Bob sounded more than half asleep already.

'No, but I'll take it as read. See you in the morning!'

Thanks to Bob's sleepiness, she was down by the

gates in plenty of time for seven-twenty, though as she stood there it seemed as though the entire hospital staff walked past and noticed her waiting. But as luck would have it, at the moment when Gerard leaned out of a taxi and beckoned to her, no one else was around to see her nipping inside the vehicle.

'Hello, Jenny!' He gave her hand a quick squeeze. 'Parking in central London's no joke, so I've dispensed with the car for this evening.'

'Lovely! It's the height of luxury for us tube-travellers to see the light of day on London,' Jenny said, settling herself comfortably against the leather upholstery. 'Isn't it a lovely evening? I pondered over bringing an umbrella, just in case, but I decided against it and I'm glad, now.'

'So am I. I don't fancy being dug sharply in the ribs with the thing if I so much as hold your hand.'

The taxi drew up outside a large West End cinema while Jenny was still pondering his last remark. She wondered uneasily if it meant that he was a cinema groper and that she would spend the entire performance fighting off clutching hands. If so, that umbrella might have come in useful despite the fine evening.

When they took their places in the back row of the circle she wondered again, but her worries were soon laid to rest. To be sure, when the lights went out he took her hand, but it appeared that this was the extent of his cinema activities, for once the big film started neither his attention nor hers wandered from the screen.

In the interval, over two large tub ice-creams, Jenny, glancing at him, got a sudden fit of the giggles. She tried to disguise it, spooning hastily away at her ice, but he turned to her, one brow rising.

'What's so funny, Jen? Have I got ice-cream on my nose?'

'No, it's just me, being silly.' He continued to look his enquiry and she giggled again. 'The truth is, it seems so incongruous to be sitting in the back row of the circle eating ice-cream with a con-consultant!' Her voice wavered and she was off again, exploding into giggles. 'I'm sorry, I'm being silly, but I've never really thought consultants were that human.'

'*If you prick us, do we not bleed? If you tickle us, do we not laugh?* I trust you recognise those immortal words and see the aptness of the quotation?'

'Yes, of course, it's *The Merchant of Venice*, and of course I know that you're just like other men because on Sunday . . . I'm sorry, that was tactless. I'm not doing very well, am I?' The lights began to dim again and Jenny turned back to the screen with a sigh of relief. 'Thank heavens for that, and I'm sorry I got the giggles.'

This time, when he held her hand, Jenny found it even more comfortable and natural than before, and when the lights came up he released her fingers with a natural tactfulness which Jenny found very reassuring. He really was an ideal escort, both civilised and sensible, and so handsome and personable that it seemed almost too good to be true!

Outside the cinema he hailed a taxi, gave the driver directions, and then joined her on the back seat, taking her hand once more.

'Well? It was a good film, wasn't it? Not just because it reaped so many awards but because it was so very well made.'

'Yes, it was good, but although I enjoyed it, it didn't altogether fit in with the picture of Gandhi and India and the British Raj that I learned at school. So enjoyment doesn't blind me to a certain bias.'

'Clever girl!' His glance was admiring. 'You're right, but it was good cinema, even if the characters were not shown warts and all. And now for a meal to round off a nice evening.'

The taxi drew up in a quiet side street and the surgeon got out, helped Jenny to alight, and paid the man off.

'Come along, it's just around the corner, and easier to cut through than to try to guide a taxi-driver round the one-way system.'

'I don't mind walking,' Jenny assured him. 'I like it. I don't get enough exercise in town. Where is this place we're going to have dinner, though? It all seems delightfully quiet and uncommercial.'

They were in a mews, with quaint old tiled cottages, obviously expensively converted into small houses with garages beneath the main living quarters. Each cottage had a tiny, stamp-sized front garden and the street itself was cobbled.

'It is. We're heading for number seven. It's my home. I thought I'd show you how domesticated I can be, so I've ordered a Chinese meal to be delivered in about twenty minutes. However, to further prove my versatility I've put a bottle of white wine in the fridge to cool and set my coffee percolator at the correct angle on the stove.' He glanced down at her in the faint light from a street lamp which resembled an old gas light. 'All right? You aren't nervous of bachelor abodes?'

He had his key in the door, but he did not open it, waiting for her reply. She knew, suddenly, that if she had said she *was* nervous he would, with perfect good temper, have taken her back to the main road and to a restaurant, which would be ridiculous with a perfectly good Chinese meal on order. Besides, she was not nervous, she was longing to see his home!

'No, of course I'm not nervous,' Jenny said, passing him as he held the green painted door open for her to do so. 'I think you're terribly lucky to have this dear little house in this charming spot. Do you share with anyone else, or is it all yours?'

She thought there was the tiniest of pauses before he intimated that he was the sole owner of the place, but she could have been mistaken and, anyway, it was soon forgotten as she went up the stairs. They were old, low-ceilinged stairs, and there were blackened beams with horse brasses on, and a bunch of dried flowers at the top, where a small landing was carpeted in dark green and empty save for a coat rack, a half-moon table with a white telephone on it, and another low table of silkily polished wood with a chrysanthemum in a pot in the middle of it. She glanced round at the doors, then back to him.

'Which one's the kitchen, Gerard?'

'First on your right. Go in and we'll get that coffee perking. I'll show you all round later.'

Jenny opened the door and found herself in a dream kitchen. It was floored with honey-gold tiles and the fittings were in pale pine, giving it a Devonshire farm-house look which was accentuated by the curtains, cream with brown and gold leaves all over them, and by the old-fashioned dresser with its burden of pleasantly varied china. But the split-level cooker, in brown and cream, was as modern as anything Jenny had ever seen. The curved breakfast bar with its leather-topped stools and a wooden tub with a small but beautiful beech tree growing in it, showed that this room had been planned, not by some kitchen-expert, but by someone with a very individual taste which he could afford to put into practice.

'Crumbs, what a perfect room!'

The words escaped her without a moment's thought and Gerard came through the doorway after her and smiled. He was obviously gratified by her immediate and patently honest response.

'Yes, it's nice, isn't it? I spend a lot of time in here one way and another, so I wanted it to suit my requirements. But that didn't mean it had to be utilitarian. There's no dining-room. I opted for a big kitchen instead, so I have to eat in here even when I'm entertaining!'

Jenny ran envious eyes over the cooker, the lovely clean working surfaces and the comfortable chairs which were drawn up to the round pine dining-table.

'And you've made it just right. Cooking must be a pleasure in a kitchen like this. Oh, was that the bell?'

He turned and went out of the kitchen, calling over his shoulder as he went. 'Yes—must be our Chinese meal. A bit early, but nonetheless welcome. Light the gas under the percolator would you?'

Jenny lit the gas, admired the percolator, which was an old-fashioned one with a heavy glass lid through which, when it began to bubble, it would be possible to see the coffee perking. Then she turned to the table, seeing that it was set for two with large, practical place mats in red and white checked gingham. She found the fridge, which was not easy since it had a pine door, and got out the bottle of wine and set it on the table, then looked around to see what else she could do just as the kitchen door opened again and Gerard came through, carrying two of those little brown carrier bags so beloved of Chinese take-aways.

'Here we are. Would you like to get the plates out of the top oven, the one by the sink? I put them in on a very low heat to keep warm. I hate eating off cold plates. Then you can dispense from this bag and I'll do the other. If there's anything you hate, holler and I'll leave it off, and if there's any over, I'll leave it until it's cold, put it in the fridge, and have it for my breakfast tomorrow. Unless Isabel wants it, of course.'

'Isabel?'

He grinned at her, carefully spooning out fried pork, Hong Kong-style, on to two plates.

'Oh dear, I hoped you'd rise to the bait and sound curious and indignant, not merely placidly interested! Hang on, she'll come running when she smells prawns, she adores them.'

He continued to dish up but presently, Jenny heard a tiny sound outside the door. And so did her companion, for he laid his spoon carefully down on a plate and went over and opened the kitchen door.

'Here she is, the woman in my life! Don't you dare jump up to the table, you uncouth animal. Stay on the floor where you belong.'

'Oh!' gasped Jenny. 'Oh, what a beautiful lady!'

The beautiful lady was, in fact, a white cat. Very small, very solemn, with huge golden eyes and a tiny pink nose, she sat herself neatly down on the floor by Gerard's feet and gazed hopefully table-wards.

'Yes, that's Isabel. I tell her she'll go yellow and get slit eyes if she keeps guzzling Chinese food, but she doesn't seem to give a damn. Here, we'd better give her some now or we'll get no peace. She's quite shameless about begging, so don't be deceived by her aristocratic looks.' He walked over to the dresser and got down a deep blue saucer which he put on the table. 'If we fill that, she will stagger out, replete, and give us some peace.'

'What does she like, apart from shrimps?' Jenny said, looking doubtfully at the delicious array of foil dishes. 'How about some beef in black bean sauce?'

'Anything. Sometimes I think she must have worms the size of serpents to eat all she does and never put on an ounce,' Gerard said. 'When you consider that she hardly gets any real exercise it's a miracle she isn't as fat as Nurse Hopkins.'

'Nurse Hopkins is a large lady,' Jenny admitted. 'Where does Isabel go when she does get exercise?'

'Go? Oh, for exercise! She goes to the park with me, on a lead, I'm ashamed to admit. I only ever take her at dead of night, mind you, because I feel such a fool. And of course she has the run of the Mews—that's a joke, when I think about it!—only she's not an outdoor cat. She stays indoors by choice all day while I'm working, though I always leave the little window in the garage open so she can get out, and I've a cat-door into the flat.'

Jenny, chuckling, sat down and sprinkled soy sauce over her well-piled plate.

'You're a cat-lover, then? Unusual, for a man, I'd have thought.'

Across the table he scowled at her, then switched his scowl to the cat, voraciously eating from her blue saucer.

'Me? A cat-lover? Now that I do resent! This skinny waif was wished on me by a Dr Ahmed at the hospital, or should I blame his wife? A nice couple, except that they had to return to their homeland about a year ago, and since they had just adopted a stray kitten and hoped to return to this country very shortly, they asked me to take care of Isabel.'

'I see. Only they haven't yet returned?'

'Nor will. Ahmed got a consultancy and his wife's running a clinic for underprivileged babies, so their plates are full for the next few years. With the utmost reluctance, therefore, I've let the wretched Isabel remain. Until I tire of her, of course.'

'Naturally. Just as though she were a woman,' Jenny said a trifle waspishly. He raised his brows, then grinned ruefully.

'Get on with your food, woman. I can hear the percolator starting to bubble.'

'I'm so full I doubt if I can move a step,' Jenny said, pushing back her plate at last. 'Still, as the washing-up is minimal I'll roll myself to the sink and get it cleared away. You make mouth-watering coffee, too.'

'Yes, it's good, isn't it? I'd back my old-fashioned percolator against one of the modern ones any day of the week. Here, I'll wipe up for you. I haven't yet bothered with a dish-washer since, when I'm alone, it's only a plate and a cup.'

The washing-up was minimal and in five minutes they were finished and Gerard was carrying a tray with more coffee on it through the door which led, he informed her over his shoulder, into the living-room. Jenny followed him and paused on the threshold while her companion stood the coffee tray down on a little table and then turned to her.

'Like it?'

'It's very nice,' Jenny said slowly. The carpet was some sort of pale fawn colour and the curtains were cream-coloured velvet to match an immense couch and the two matching armchairs. The lighting came from two wall sconces, both shaded in dark red so that the amount of actual radiance was a sort of dull pinky glow.

'You're not keen!' He sounded surprised but not hurt. 'What don't you care for?'

'It's all very nice, it's just not the sort of room I expected,' Jenny said with what lightness she could muster. In truth, she thought the room seemed far too like a love-nest! 'It's not at all like the rest of the house—what I've seen of it, I mean.'

She had gone to the bathroom to wash her hands before sitting down to the meal. It was a lovely room with a sunken bath and pale green tiles decorated with pictures of golden clumps of bamboo. They looked so real that she almost expected the delicate fronds to rustle in the breeze. And the spare room, where Isabel held sway, was a study equipped with a large desk, two equally large and comfortable easy chairs, a blue cat-basket with a blanket and a scratching board which Isabel seemed, by the state of it, to use with vigour.

'Less practical, I suppose,' he murmured. He took her hand and led her over to the couch. 'But I want comfort in here more than severe practicality.'

She sat down beside him and aknowledged the comfort of the soft, cream-coloured cushions while he poured their coffee and handed her a cup.

'Drink that up and you shall have a liqueur. What would you like? I've got Tia Maria, Cointreau, Benedictine . . . You can choose, presently.'

'Nothing, thanks. I'm not much of a drinker. But you have one if you feel like it.'

'No, I'm not that keen.' He began to sip his coffee. 'Now, since I'm not drinking liqueurs, you can entertain me. Tell me your life-story.'

'It's short and rather dull,' Jenny demurred. 'We well-brought-up girls are always dull.'

'Well, tell me about your modelling career,' the surgeon suggested. 'I expect it was hard work, but to a dull and hidebound hospital consultant it will all seem very glamorous.'

'I did model—I still do, a bit. How did you find out? It isn't something I talk about much. I suppose it was that travel poster in the underground station!'

'No, I read your file.' He raised one black brow at her indignant squeak. 'Why not? It's one of the few privileges of rank that I can check my girlfriends out if they happen to be on the staff.'

'At least you're honest.'

Jenny glanced at him, beside her on the couch. He had turned so that he could watch her as she talked and his eyes were half-closed, his mouth half-smiling. He looked like a man hoping to be amused by what he was about to hear, which was rather daunting, since Jenny intended to keep all the embarrassing moments in her life strictly to herself. However, she gave him a brief resume of her modelling career.

'When I first started I belonged to an agency and they sent me out on various assignments. I modelled clothing and shoes in the big stores, and fur coats for a very exclusive place in Mayfair one Christmas. I've done photographic work, too, for magazines and for advertisements, and I've appeared with horrid briefness on television. Mainly, to be honest, as an earlobe with a diamond drop sparkling on it, or an ankle with a gold chain and a fashionable court shoe. But once or twice the whole me was filmed and actually appeared. I did a stint at the Motor Show, but that's pretty amateur stuff—you wear a bikini and lie around on the bonnet of a Ford Bambini or whatever, and elderly men pretend they're interested in the car to get a closer look at your legs. There was the odd occasion when someone made a pass, or even when someone very nice on a magazine or in a firm took you out to dinner, but it was pretty dull really. A lot duller than nursing.'

The surgeon finished his coffee, put down the cup, and then put an arm round Jenny's shoulders, pulling her close to him.

'Well, if it was that dull we won't talk at all,' he murmured. 'Come a bit closer. Actions speak louder than words.'

His mouth covered hers, lightly at first and then more urgently, while his hands slid beneath her blouse. Jenny's love-life had always worked on a sort of slide-rule system, so this should have been permissible, only her heart began to beat unevenly and his expert, tantalising caresses filled her with a longing stronger than any she had experienced before. She knew, vaguely, that her slide-rule system was going to be no use in this situation, that she had never before found herself making love with a man whose sexual attraction—and undoubted expertise—had already marked him as the dominant partner in their relationship. Usually it was she who set the limits, she who broke the embrace, and it had always been because she wanted to stop the man's advances.

This time, she had no desire whatsoever to call a halt. She moaned as his hands crept round her, crushing her closer to him. She felt herself pushed gently back against the cream-coloured cushions and then he was lifting her, and because her arms were by now locked round his neck he was free to move away any of her clothing which impeded their love-making. It was only when cool air touched her body that she began to struggle, feeling his mouth move from hers, travelling down to the base of her throat, his kisses urgent, demanding.

'Stop it!' Her voice was sufficiently vehement to make him raise his head.

'Stop what? Stop kissing you?'

He sounded amused and, infuriatingly, completely in command of himself. Jenny, all too aware that her own self-control was at a very low ebb, began to pull herself together. She struggled into a sitting position, began to button up her blouse and then spoke, fighting to make her voice sound as cool and amused as his.

'If you just stop, Gerard, that'll do for now. It must be fairly obvious that I enjoy it, but only up to a point. In other words, I'm not searching for a casual affair. So are you going to take me home in the car, or will you ring for a taxi, or shall I walk?'

He tutted, wagging a chiding finger at her.

'Temper, temper! Don't you like being seduced on a comfortable couch? Would you rather move through to the bedroom, do the thing properly?'

That really did bring a flash to Jenny's eyes. The cheek of the man! She finished buttoning her blouse, pulled her skirt, which was inexplicably back-to-front, round the right way, and then gave her companion the coldest look at her command.

'Don't be silly, Gerard. I want to go home now.'

He shrugged, lying back against the cushions, watching her through lazily slitted eyelids.

'Why should you want to go home? My dear girl, you've been around. Don't pretend you've never slept with one of your numerous boyfriends because I wouldn't believe you. Everyone at the hospital knows you're very hot stuff and . . .'

This time it took no effort to put loathing and scorn into her glance. A man of his experience and intelligence could not possibly give a moment's credence to hospital gossip! He was just using it, hoping to make her more vulnerable to what, at first, she had thought a very poor sort of joke!

'Don't pretend you believe even half the things they say about people at work! Just because I've been a model, that doesn't mean I've gone to bed with half of London. Photographers and businessmen wouldn't get far if they spent all their time chasing girls. I won't pretend I wasn't propositioned, because of course I was, and of course I turned them all down. I don't intend to get married until I'm twenty-five, I *told* you that, and I don't want affairs with anyone, no matter how exalted. Anyway, what sort of a mockery would it make of our working relationship if I thought of you as a—a lover and not a surgeon? If two people fall in love that's one thing, but just to go to bed because of a strong physical attraction—well, it creates chaos and I like a tidy life. Is that clear?'

'As crystal.' He put his arm round her, gently this time, and swung her to face him. He looked contrite, she was relieved to see. 'I accept your argument and I apologise for leaping to conclusions. I dare say the story that you'd posed in the nude for batteries of cameras . . .' he gave her a little squeeze as she turned furiously on him, scarlet-cheeked. 'All right, I'm sorry, I was only repeating what had been said to me! But even so, I want to take you out, for the pleasure of your company and because we really do get on well. Am I allowed to hope that you won't leap away every time I kiss you, though? You see, it's only by kissing you that I'll bring you round to a more liberal point of view, regarding love-making.'

'I only leap away, as you put it, when I feel things

are rapidly getting out of hand. Out of my hand,' Jenny said honestly. 'I've enjoyed my evening very much, otherwise.' She glanced at her watch. 'Heavens, I must go, it's awfully late. Could you ring for a taxi?'

He lounged to his feet, then turned and pulled her up as well.

'I'm taking you to your door in the car, so don't try to prove how independent you can be. When are you next off at a weekend?'

'In a month. Why? Do you often go back to Bath?'

'Not often, but if you're going down in a month it would be an idea to combine our trip again, don't you think? I've found that a good deal of enjoyment can be gained from just being in your company.'

'That would be lovely. And thank you for being so understanding about my . . . my rules. I don't mean to be a prig, but I have to have certain standards.'

He smiled and tilted her face to his.

'Very understandable, but they won't last. You're far too beautiful to remain single and unattached.' His mouth hovered, but just before he kissed her he said, 'All right, Jenny?'

It was a lovely, bone-melting kiss, the sort of kiss that has a girl thinking of throwing her inhibitions to the four winds, but Jenny clung grimly to hers and broke the kiss while she was still able.

It was awful the way her careful rules kept biting the dust one by one! First the 'no doctors' had gone, then the 'no kissing on a first date' had been calmly brushed aside the very first time Gerard had driven her home, and now the 'no cuddling when you're alone with him' had crashed. And she knew in her heart the very strictest rule of all had absolutely teetered on the brink of being abandoned.

She had clung to it, all right, but she knew, in her heart, how near she had been to letting that rule go overboard. No one, in five happy years of dating men, had ever made her wish, even for a moment, that she could break it, but Gerard Sterne had very nearly caused her to regret her own firmness.

'No coat? Then we'd better get moving, I suppose.'

'Thanks for a marvellous evening, Gerard, and for being very understanding. Where's Isabel?'

He took her elbow, to lead her down the stairs and into the garage where his silver-grey sports car stood alone.

'Isabel? Oh, she's out on the tiles. She spends most of the night out in the Mews. It's quiet and there isn't much traffic. It's just day-times when she tends to stay indoors.' He opened the passenger door of the car and then pressed a button. The garage door purred softly upward as he went round and slid behind the wheel. 'There, now we'll not let the engine do more than whisper until we're out of earshot of my neighbours. I don't want complaints.'

Jenny never let boyfriends take her all the way home because she had done so once or twice and had got sick of the 'what's a nice girl like you living in a dump like this?' routine. She had also suspected that her escorts got a wrong impression when the chuckers-out and the manager and even some of the clients of the amusement arcade greeted her so casually. At the end of Byron Road, within a stone's throw of the arcade, was a small block of modern flats built round a central courtyard. The girls could slip into the tunnel-like passageway which led into the courtyard one side, and then either linger in the darkness until their escort had driven off or, if the back gate was open, go through it, along a very short side street lined with dustbins, and emerge a little further down the road.

Tonight, however, the gate would be closed, so Jenny got out, thanked Gerard for the lift, and then headed for the tunnel. She waited until the sound of his car had faded into silence and then came back on to the road and set off for the flat.

CHAPTER FOUR

'MORNING, Nurse!' Sandra greeted Jenny as they met outside the office, then held the door open for her so that they could both enter the room together. 'Did you enjoy the film?'

'Yes, very much,' Jenny said. 'I didn't say anything earlier, but I went with Mr Sterne and afterwards we had dinner together.'

Sandra's eyebrows shot up.

'Gracious! He's good company though, so why not? But I got you to come in here first thing because today's going to be one of those days and I thought the earlier we started sorting things out the better. We've got two definite morning admissions for surgery later today, one admission for observation—a suspected duodenal ulcer—and another chap who was booked in for theatre but who has cancelled the actual operation today, though he's hoping to make it here later.'

'I see. Which rooms are they going in?' Jenny frowned. 'So far as I can remember, there are only three rooms vacant, though one of them's a double, of course. But didn't you say that private patients don't usually care for sharing?'

'That's just it, they don't. But I've been wondering, since we're so full and we really like to keep a room clear for emergencies, whether Miss Stott and Mrs Franklyn would share? You know them better than I do.'

'I think they'd jump at it,' Jenny said honestly. 'It's lucky that they're both orthopaedic, too, which would mean that when Ger . . . Mr Sterne comes to see one he can see the other as well. Yes, I'm sure it would work. Do you want me to mention it when I do obs?'

'If you would. I shouldn't think it will be until tomorrow, and do tell them that the double room is a lot cheaper than the singles, though they're both covered by insurance schemes, so that probably won't bother them. Incidentally, can you cope with the two admissions who are in the waiting-room? Gillian will give you a hand, I know.'

'Yes, of course. Can I have the details?' Jenny took the charts and the folders and glanced down at them. 'A woman for a tonsillectomy and a chap with exostosis of the hallux. What's that when it's at home?'

'A bunion,' Sandra said briefly. 'You wouldn't think it would be much, but it's quite a nasty operation to get over. He'll be in a week. Dishy chap, too. I bet he hasn't told his girlfriend what he's in here for; bunions sound so elderly!'

'Right, I'll process them through the system and then do obs.' Jenny waved the folder, left the office and headed down the corridor to the waiting-room. She was still pleased with herself over the successful conclusion to her evening. Gerard was nice, despite being a member of the despised medical profession, and she was looking forward to seeing him again, both socially and during working hours. His appearance, she told herself airily as she opened the door of the waiting-room, was definitely dream-material. She had been very fortunate to attract his notice.

'Good morning,' she said cheerfully to the two occupants of the room, then stopped short, her mouth dropping open. 'Oh!'

The woman who smiled at her over the top of a magazine was slim, dark, middle-aged, with rather a lot of lipstick on and an air of bravado which probably masked a good deal of nervousness. But it was the man who had drawn that involuntary exclamation from Jenny's lips. Tall and undeniably handsome, with thickly waving chestnut-coloured hair and reddish-brown eyes, he got to his feet as she entered and stared at her very hard. Then he smiled slowly. It was not a pleasant smile.

'Miss Speed! Whatever are you doing here, Jenny? Apart from masquerading as a nurse, I mean.'

'I am a nurse, Mr Whelpton,' Jenny said stiffly. She turned to the other patient. 'Mrs Sayers? Would you come with me, please?' She turned back to Mr Whelpton. 'I shan't be long, sir.'

Heart hammering, she led Mrs Sayers to her room, turned down the bed and asked her to change into her nightdress and then to ring the bell beside the pillows so that her details could be filled in on the chart. At this point she should have returned to the waiting-room for the other patient, but instead she hurried to Sister's office. She shot open the door after the most perfunctory of knocks and Sandra, writing steadily, looked up.

'You're soon back, Jenny. Anything the matter?'

'Everything. I know Mr Whelpton—rather too well for comfort! Sandy, he's a vile man. He owns a chain of boutiques and he markets his own designs. I've done some work for him. He's the sort of chap who thinks a model can be bought and who gets very nasty when you tell him he's mistaken. We had a fearful row over . . . Well, anyway, I really don't think I ought to do the admission.'

Sandra pulled a face and pushed her cap on to the back of her head.

'You're right, but it's going to make things difficult. Not now, of course, Gillian can do the admission, but later. He'll be in five days, by the way, not a whole week.' She smiled at Jenny. 'But it'll feel like a week, I expect, if you dislike him as much as you seem to. Incidentally, Mr Sterne's coming round early today since he's doing the bunionectomy first.'

'Oh, crumbs, then I'd better get the obs over so I can do the ward round,' Jenny said, heading back towards the door. 'Thanks a million, Sandra, for being so understanding about Doggy. I'll work twice as hard to make up.'

'Right . . .' Sandra, about to start work again, did a double-take. 'What did you say his name was?'

Jenny laughed.

'Douglas, actually, only most of the girls call him Doggy. It's only appropriate if you know him well.'

'Hmm.' Sandra sighed and stood up. 'I'll go and fish Gillian out of Mr Robson's room and get her going on Mr Whelpton. You'll see Miss Stott and Mrs Franklyn about the possibility of sharing a room?'

'I will,' Jenny said as the two of them emerged into the corridor. 'They'll jump at it, you see.'

They did. Both ladies viewed the prospect with enthusiasm, though Miss Stott was very anxious that Jenny should not forget that today was her great day.

'My brother-in-law will bring Baby to the back hall, just as you said, dear, at four o'clock, after visiting on the ordinary wards,' she said as soon as Jenny had wound the sphygmomanometer round her arm. 'Sister said it would be all right, but that you would be seeing Mr Sterne about it, just to make sure. Have you spoken to him yet?'

'Not yet. But I'll do it before the ward round starts,' Jenny promised, deftly slipping the thermometer into Miss Stott's open mouth. 'I don't think there's any question of you being moved today; it's operating day and we're terribly rushed, but you can look forward to having company from tomorrow if everything goes according to plan.'

It was, as Sister had said, one of those mornings. After she had finished charting the progress of all the patients Jenny hurried up the corridor, arriving in Sister's office just as Mr Sterne turned into the ward. He and his team would have headed straight for their first patient, but Jenny called him.

'Mr Sterne—I wonder if you could spare a minute?'

'Go ahead, Nat,' Mr Sterne said indicating the already open door of Room Two. 'I'll join you very shortly.' To Jenny, he added, 'Well, Nurse?'

'We're rather full, sir, so Sister wondered whether it would be all right to put Miss Stott and Mrs Franklyn in one of the double rooms. I've spoken to them and they're both very keen.'

'Right, fine. Anything else?'

'Well, Miss Stott's brother-in-law is bringing her Baby into the hospital this afternoon, after visiting. Will it be all right if he comes on to the ward? I believe he's very good, probably a lot less trouble than most visitors.'

Mr Sterne raised an eyebrow at her, a half-smile on his face.

'Why on earth not? There's no time limit for visiting on the private ward, you know.' The smile broadened. 'You just wanted an excuse to get me alone, admit it!'

He stepped towards her, a hand taking her chin, just as the door to Room Two opened again and Nat Phillips headed towards them. The surgeon turned to face his registrar.

'Done already? Right, I'd better just pop my head round the door.'

Jenny, following the team meekly, knew that this would be a quick round, more to reassure the patients than anything, since the consultant was due in the operating theatre very shortly. She hoped that all would go well—and it did, until they entered Mr Whelpton's room. He was in an operating gown, she was relieved to see, and sitting on his bed, but the moment he laid eyes on her he got to his feet, gave a well-simulated cry of surprise, and grabbed her firmly round the waist. Before she could do much more than squeak he had kissed her smack on the mouth.

'Darling Jenny, wonderful to see you,' he said enthusiastically. He turned to the consultant. 'Almost prettier in uniform than out of it wouldn't you say, Mr Sterne?'

Jenny, pulling herself free, knew that her face was scarlet with embarrassment and knew, also, that Douglas Whelpton had set out to cause her as much mortification as possible. How well he had succeeded! She shot a glance at Gerard, who was looking both startled and angry.

'Mr Whelpton, I'd be grateful if you'd treat my nurse with more respect in future, please.'

'Respect?' Douglas Whelpton grinned. '*Your* nurse? She was my little Jenny long before she became your nurse, Mr Sterne.' There was a wealth of salacious meaning in Mr Whelpton's voice and Jenny squirmed. 'Many's the good time I've had with little Jenny, eh, Jen?'

'I can't recall ever being happy in your company,' Jenny said icily. 'When does Mr Whelpton go to theatre, sir?'

But Douglas Whelpton, bent on making as much mischief as possible, was undeterred.

'What about Hastings, Jenny? What a night that was!'

He laughed on a low, intimate note. 'And what a tissue of lies I had to tell Felix next morning, when he found some of your frillies in the back of the Stingray!'

Before Jenny could get a word out, Mr Sterne had intervened. He looked ominous.

'That's quite enough thank you, Mr Whelpton. Nurse, get this patient on to the bed for examination.'

Jenny swung Mr Whelpton's feet up into the air with enough vicious force to crash his head heavily on to the pillow, but much she cared! If the creature had any brains, they'd be well and truly curdled by now, she thought, hauling off his bedroom slipper and very nearly performing the bunionectomy with the hard leather edge of the instep, judging by her patient's hissing intake of breath. She caught his toes firmly and twisted the foot so that the bulge of the bunion faced the surgeon.

'There, sir.'

'That,' hissed the patient vehemently, 'is the wrong bloody foot!'

'Oh!' Jenny said, momentarily crestfallen. 'But that's a bunion.'

'True, Nurse,' said Mr Sterne. He seemed to be having some difficulty in keeping a straight face. 'But it isn't particularly large or particularly painful. Try the other foot.'

'It's all right,' Mr Whelpton began. 'I can . . .'

He got no further. Jenny had removed his slipper and turned his foot sideways with even more speed and efficiency than before. This time his eyes widened and his cheeks paled as the slipper was snatched off, but he did not actually emit a sound. He was, she realised, holding his breath.

'That's the fellow.' Mr Sterne was calling attention to the size and splendour of the bunion and telling his houseman at some length how he intended to deal with it.

'This deformity has been caused by the wearing of a too-small and too-tight shoe,' he began. Jenny saw the patient's eyes widen indignantly at the word deformity. 'Conservative treatment has already proved useless and so surgery is vital. The exostosis will be cut away, and though many surgeons use plaster fixation followed by pulp traction with nylon sutures, I favour bandaging the foot so that the big toe is held in the varus position. We'll start exercise on the third day and Mr Whelpton can get about a bit with the aid of crutches. He can go home . . . when, Dr Meakins?'

'On the fifth or sixth day, sir, if the wound begins to heal as it ought,' the houseman said eagerly. 'Back to the ward for suture removal after a fortnight, and then weight-bearing can commence.'

'Good. Nurse Speed, you'll see that Mr Whelpton does the foot exercises I shall give him? And you'll teach him to walk properly when he comes in for suture removal. Is that all clear?'

'Certainly, sir,' Jenny murmured. She gave the now wilting patient a sweet, forgiving smile. 'I think Mr Whelpton will find the exercises very . . . very stimulating.'

From his unheroic position, Mr Whelpton managed an icy glare before the team, and Jenny, left him.

Outside, however, Mr Sterne waved the team on and then turned to Jenny.

'What was all that about? Hastings? And frillies in his car? Nurse Speed, have you been up to something with that unsavoury specimen?'

'Certainly not. I worked for him once and left after a blazing row, and I thought he'd make me feel uncomfortable.' Jenny giggled. 'That was why I dealt with him so briskly.'

'I noticed. Just remember that he's a private patient, will you? He's entitled to a degree of respect.'

'So am I,' Jenny pointed out. 'He behaved awfully badly, sir.'

'I know. That was why I didn't reprimand you for whipping his slipper off so fast that his sole smoked,' Mr Sterne said. 'You're *sure* you didn't . . .'

'No! I didn't! Really I didn't!'

'Hmm. Doth the lady protest too much, I ask myself? No, it's all right, only joking. Come along, Nurse, next patient!'

The day continued at a hectic pace. Patients went down to theatre and returned, meals were eaten, blood samples taken, and a Very Important Lady, in for a hysterectomy, suddenly decided that she did not want to have the operation after all. It took all Dr Mongresin's considerable charm and all the persuasive powers of Jenny and Sandra to get the lady into a sufficiently co-operative frame of mind to allow herself to be prepped for theatre. Indeed, Dr Mongresin, with a nightmare vision, he told Jenny later, of his boss gowned, sterile and empty-handed, descended in the end to subterfuge.

'Just a little injection, Lady St Clair, to calm you,' he said soothingly, giving the patient his most charming smile. 'After all, even if you decide not to have the operation we don't want you lying awake all night because your nerves have been overstressed.'

Jenny, listening, could only admire the aplomb with which he spoke and the speed with which he hustled his suddenly lethargic and acquiescent patient on to the waiting trolley.

'What did you give her?' she hissed as they descended together in the lift. Pierre smiled blindingly at her.

'Oh, a mere nothing, just a little shot of . . .' he gave her a comical look, '. . . what's the name of it in English? I can't remember!'

In view of all this, it was scarcely surprising that Jenny returned to the ward with the next patient to come up and realised with a shock that it was four o'clock. Indecisively she glanced up the corridor to Miss Stott's room; should she rush up there and just confirm that the brother-in-law was arriving? But it was silly, when she could nip down in the lift and see for herself. Hospital rules being what they were, it was unlikely that there would be more than one man with a little dog sitting in the back hall, though even if there were half-a-dozen, she still had a tongue in her head and could enquire which one was Baby Stott.

Accordingly, she hurried down to the lift and got into it. When she reached the ground floor she stepped out and glanced across the back hall, then stopped short, disbelief widening her eyes. That could not be Baby, surely? An Alsatian the size of a donkey stood patiently beside a small man with greying hair who sat on a leather-covered seat reading a paperback. As Jenny walked forward the man saw her and rose to his feet.

'Nurse Speed? Here's the old fellow, Nurse. He's a good lad. I'll just wait here and read my book until you're ready to bring him back. About thirty minutes be enough?'

'Er . . . yes, definitely,' Jenny stammered, taking the thick plait of leather which was looped around the dog's massive neck. 'This *is* Baby, I take it? Baby Stott, I mean?'

The man looked surprised. 'This is Baby, all right.

Big, isn't he?' He chuckled, ruffling the dog's thick neck-fur. 'Soft as a lamb, Baby is though, despite his size. Just you keep hold of the lead, Nurse, and he'll give you no trouble. He's more obedient than many a child and he does love our Mavis!'

'Yes, I'm sure,' Jenny murmured, remembering that Miss Stott was indeed called Mavis. She tugged on the lead and her huge charge followed her meekly towards the lift. 'I'll be back in half an hour, then.'

Baby had not previously been in a lift. He entered without a qualm but disapproved strongly of the door shutting on him. He glanced nervously at Jenny as if he suspected that, finding him alone, the temptation to take advantage of him in some way might prove too much for her. Jenny, harbouring similar suspicions in reverse, for the lift was small and Baby's teeth large, smiled placatingly at him and smoothed the fur between his ears.

'Aren't you a lovely fellow, then? Soon you'll be seeing Mummy.'

Miss Stott had confided that she always referred to herself as Mummy when talking to the dog, and Jenny had no wish to alienate her companion by letting him see she thought this pretty silly. There was nothing silly about an Alsatian which weighed upwards of ten stone! The lift stopped, Jenny and Baby stepped out, and Jenny made straight for Miss Stott's room. She knocked briefly and entered, her fingers slackening on the lead as she approached the bed.

'There's Mummy, Baby! Miss Stott, Baby's come to see you!'

Rather to Jenny's surprise, Miss Stott was lying down in her bed facing the far wall, but as Jenny spoke she stirred, and as she stirred Baby, catching the word

'Mummy', launched himself at the bed like a large and furry rocket. One moment he was in the air and the person in the bed was turning, the next the person in the bed was on his back and Baby had landed squarely on the man's . . . well, the man's anatomy, Jenny told herself defensively, as a roar split the air. But . . . a *man*? In Miss Stott's bed?

'Baby! Get off! I'm sorry, but what on earth are you doing in Miss Stott's bed?'

It was a confusing moment. A fair-haired man in his thirties lay, red-faced and gasping, looking up at Jenny while Baby, thoroughly demoralised, backed uneasily towards the door, towing Jenny behind him.

The man leaned up on his elbow. He was clutching his middle, still gasping for breath.

'Who . . . who?'

Jenny began to explain but as the first words left her lips the door opened behind her and Baby, seeing his chance, tore out into the corridor with Jenny lashing helplessly from side to side, too firmly attached to the looped lead to let go. She registered that the door had been opened by Nurse Roach, pushing a trolley, that nurse, trolley and various other objects now strewed the corridor—but not until she was too far away to do more than shout a breathless apology over her shoulder.

Baby, apparently hearing the apology and believing it to be a command, stopped so short that Jenny collided with him, sufficiently forcefully for the dog to utter a grunt of protest. He gave her a hunted look and then set off down the corridor, clearly intent on escape. This lunatic asylum, the look said, was no place for a decent, respectable dog!

Their flight might have continued uninterrupted had not a group of doctors approached them. The sight of Mr

Hopwood's august white head, with Pierre Mongresin beside him and the houseman slightly to the rear, deflected Baby from his apparent intention of leaving the premises. He stopped, snuffed the air, and then attacked the nearest door with toenails which tore size-able grooves in the wood. Jenny, desperate to get out of the way before Mr Hopwood saw her properly, opened the door and slipped inside, keeping a firm hold of Baby's lead. She did not intend to allow a repetition of what had happened last time they entered a bedroom.

But there was a cry of delight from one of the two beds in the room and a sniff from the other, and then Baby had torn himself free from the lead and was once again standing on a sacred hospital bed. This time, how different his reception! Miss Stott's arms were round his neck, her thin little face was buried in his ruff, and she and Baby were both uttering little coos of pleasure.

Jenny leaned on the door, her knees weak, her limbs bruised, her fingers sore. Outside, she knew, retribution lurked, but in here all was sweetness and light, with the two old friends enjoying a marvellous reunion. It was not my fault, she reminded herself. I was only the instrument, and how could I have guessed that anyone would call a dog of that size Baby?

After a couple of minutes Miss Stott ordered her pet reluctantly off the bed and turned a radiant face to Jenny.

'Nurse, it's wonderful to see him again! Oh, what a good boy he is—Mummy's best boy!' She fished around in her bedside cabinet and produced a bar of chocolate. It was a half-pound bar but Baby swallowed it like a Malteser. Jenny realised that his excessive size could be accounted for by quite natural means and managed a weak smile. After all, she could scarcely blame Miss

Stott for never telling her how huge Baby was. Once, presumably, he had been small and sweet. To Miss Stott, he probably still seemed so.

'Yes, he's a fine fellow,' Jenny said, with what enthusiasm she could muster. 'But I'm afraid we went into your old room first. No one told me that you'd been moved today. Sister said it would be tomorrow.'

'There's been an emergency admission, I believe,' Miss Stott said vaguely. '*Clever* Baby, he found his Mummy, didn't he?'

Baby, sitting meekly by the bed, licked his lips and gazed meaningly at the bedside cabinet. Miss Stott unwrapped another chocolate bar which disappeared with equal alacrity and Mrs Franklyn, upright and disapproving in her own bed, sniffed.

'How old is that creature? Four years old? If you go on feeding him chocolate at that rate he won't have a tooth in his head by the time he's five.'

Miss Stott bridled.

'A little treat, that's all it is,' she said defensively. 'And my sister doesn't approve of giving dogs chocolate, so the poor fellow has been deprived for weeks.' She rubbed the huge head and Baby managed to take on the appearance of a dog who has been regularly starved and probably beaten like a gong into the bargain. Miss Stott beamed proudly at her pet. 'Who's a lovely boy, then?'

Jenny, leaning against the door, was about to agree that Baby was a very fine animal when the door opened sharply, canting her forward a couple of feet, and a voice spoke near her ear.

'What the devil's happening?'

Jenny turned. Mr Sterne was living up to his name. There was not the trace of a smile on his countenance. He looked very angry.

'I'm sorry, sir, there was a misunderstanding and . . .'

Mr Sterne lowered his voice, but there could be no mistaking his fury.

'Get that dog out of here and come straight to my office. Understand? Straight means at once!'

'But I'm on duty, sir, and we've had an emergency admission, which is . . .'

'Do as I say.'

The words were snapped out with enough venom to startle Jenny into a quick affirmative. Then he was gone, shutting the door decisively behind him. Jenny took hold of Baby's lead again.

'Sorry, Miss Stott, I'd better take him downstairs again now. I did tell your brother-in-law I wouldn't keep him up here longer than thirty minutes and I'm afraid the time is up.'

'I hope you won't get into trouble, Nurse,' Miss Stott said, waving goodbye to her pet. 'A thousand thanks for bringing him up, it's quite made my day!'

The sniff from the other bed sounded almost as if Mrs Franklyn, too, was sorry to see Baby go.

Jenny arrived at Mr Sterne's office a few moments later to find that he was still doing his ward round, or so she was informed by the cool and collected Janice Quinton.

'But you can wait, if you want,' she added, her eyes going disdainfully over Jenny's somewhat rumpled appearance. A struggle with Baby was no way to pristine elegance, Jenny would have been the first to admit it, but surely she could not look as awful as Janice's eyes implied?

'I'll wait,' Jenny said, trying to sound as if she had some choice in the matter. She reflected, taking a chair, that Mr Sterne had not been exaggerating when he said he kept his life compartmented. There had been nothing of Gerard in the way he had spoken to her in Miss Stott's room, and she realised that she was dreading what he would say in the sanctuary of his own office. Perhaps she should have refused to take the dog as soon as she saw how big he was? But it was no use wondering. The deed had been done and could only be regretted and apologised for.

She did not have long to wait. He came down the corridor and into Janice's small room, giving Jenny not so much as a glance. But as he passed her he said, 'In here!' in a tone which brooked neither argument nor delay. Jenny stumbled to her feet and followed him, taking the seat he pointed out. He said nothing more until he was seated in the swivel-chair behind the desk, and then he spoke with hateful coldness.

'Well? Do you realise what your stupidity has done to the Annabel Goodson Ward? Not only did you cause valuable—and sterile—medical equipment to be broken and scattered, but you let that . . . that werewolf leap on to the bed—and belly—of a sick man. A man with a suspected duodenal ulcer. The fact that he's a cabinet minister may seem of little importance to you, but it is of overriding importance to Mr Hopwood! He actually implied that it was my fault; that *I* had encouraged a patient of mine to be visited by a dog! As if I would dream of allowing a vicious brute like that on my ward!'

Jenny's head came up and her eyes met Mr Sterne's. This was too bad!

'But you did say he could come up, you know you did! I asked you and you said yes, fine!' She was about to embroider this statement when the door opened behind her and Mr Hopwood stalked into the room. He was still looking furious. He cast a contemptuous glance at Jenny, who had scrambled to her feet, but waved her to sit down again and brought another chair forward, on to which he sank.

'Well, Gerard? Have you found out just what the girl was playing at? If this was her idea of a joke—I heard all about the liver episode—then I'm getting her suspended from this moment.'

'That isn't fair, sir!' Jenny's horror of such a thing happening overcame her reluctance to speak up for herself. 'Really, it was just a series of accidents. I wouldn't dream of indulging in practical jokes on the ward.' She began to tick her reasons off on her fingers, her face as earnest as she knew how to make it. 'One, no one told me that Miss Stott had been moved, which was why I took the dog into the wrong room; two, I asked Sister's permission and Mr Sterne's before bringing the animal on to the ward, and three . . .'

She was rudely interrupted.

'*What* did you say? Are you saying that I approved this visit? And Sister Fox? Nurse Speed, you must be out of your mind!'

'But you did!' Jenny said. 'So did Sister. I *told* Sister you'd been willing, I . . .' she broke off at his expression of pure disbelief. 'Ask Sister Fox, she'll tell you!'

Sandra Fox was sent for and came briskly into the room.

'Yes, sir? I came at once but we're terribly busy without Nurse Speed, so can you be fairly brief?'

This, Jenny could see, did not improve Mr Sterne's temper. A white line showed round his mouth.

'Briefly, Sister, did you authorise Nurse Speed to bring a dog on to the ward this afternoon?'

'Yes, I did,' Sandra said firmly. 'I knew you had said it would do Miss Stott good, and . . .'

'What gave you the idea that I'd said such a thing, Sister? You aren't trying to say that you asked me about the dog, are you?'

'Well, no, I didn't mention it to you,' Sandra said, glancing rather guiltily at Jenny. 'But I knew Nurse Speed had asked you, and . . .'

This time it was Mr Hopwood who interrupted. He looked far less cross now, even a little amused.

'Obviously the whole affair was unfortunate, the result of a misunderstanding rather than a practical joke.' He turned to Jenny, his face softening into a smile. 'I'm sorry I was so fierce, Nurse, but just for a moment I really thought you might have considered it amusing to introduce that animal on to the ward.' He paused, eyeing her quizzically. 'May I ask if you knew the size of Miss Stott's pet before you brought him in?'

'No, I thought he was quite tiny or I'd never have suggested bringing him up,' Jenny admitted readily. 'In fact I was rather scared when he took off up the corridor. I'm really very sorry, sir.'

'Then it's forgotten.' He patted her shoulder and headed for the door. 'I'll see you later, Gerard, but now I think Sister and I had better return to the ward and to my patient; he's still almost speechless from the shock of having that dog on his stomach, which means that I can examine him without being lectured on politics, at any rate.'

Mr Hopwood and Sister left the room and Jenny got to her feet just as Mr Sterne, too, stood up.

'I'm sorry about it all, Gerard,' Jenny said timidly. 'But I'm sure you've remembered now that you *did* give permission for Miss Stott's . . .'

She got no further. Gerard Sterne swept past her, threw open the door and gestured her through it.

'No, Nurse, I cannot recall an event which never took place,' he said crisply. 'And I've no time for someone who won't take responsibility for their own mistakes and is prepared to lie to avoid trouble. It makes me suspect that they've lied over other things, such as why Mr Whelpton, who seems a decent and respectable man, should make accusations about carryings-on in Hastings. You'd better return to your ward now, Nurse.'

'He as good as called me a liar, and he thinks I'm the sort of person who would let someone else take the blame rather than get into trouble! I never want to see him again!' Jenny's eyes flashed with fury. 'But it was him who lied and who was afraid to admit that he'd given permission for Baby to come on the ward, not me. And what was worse, when I tried to explain all over again he virtually slammed his office door in my face. And of course, he had to say it all in the doorway, didn't he, so Janice couldn't but have heard. I'm never going to speak to him again, not if I live to be a hundred!'

It was two days later and Sister Fox and Jenny were having their coffee-break. Since the fateful day of Baby's visit, Jenny had managed to avoid Gerard Sterne, possibly helped by his equally obvious desire to avoid her. But now Sister Fox was pointing out that this attitude could not continue.

'This is a job of work, Jenny, and you're two adult people, so you must simply forget it ever happened,' she said. 'You were in the right, I'm sure of it, but I'm equally sure that it's all a mistake. Mr Sterne probably wasn't listening when you spoke to him. He was probably thinking of something else and just said yes without pausing to consider. So please, love, don't just turn round and leave a room when he walks into it another time. It's terribly obvious, terribly rude, and . . . well, he *is* a consultant.'

'All right. I'm sorry, I know you're right, really.' Jenny got up and picked up their coffee tray. 'It isn't the end of the world, but it is the end of a friendship, I'm afraid. But, we are, as you point out, still colleagues.'

'Good. And now, before you fly off with that tray, have you been in to see Mr Anderson? Mr Sterne wants him to do a bit more walking on those crutches, so if you've a moment later you might take him up and down the corridor a few times.'

'I'll do that. Anything else?'

'No, except you mustn't forget that you're coming to see my flat and have a meal with Stan and I on Friday.'

'I'm looking forward to it.'

Jenny left the office and hurried along to the kitchen to wash up the cups and coffee pot, but even though she worked quickly and efficiently, humming as she did so, she still felt sore about Mr Sterne's accusations. What was worse, though she had not mentioned it to Sandra, he had made it crystal clear that he now believed all the spiteful things that Doggy had said about her.

She remembered the Hastings incident with horror still. She had gone down to do a mannequin show of boutique clothes and had found, on arrival, that Doggy Whelpton had booked them into the hotel as a married couple. She had completed the show, since her agent had booked her for it, and had been forced to abandon her belongings in Doggy's Stingray and take the train back to London. He had not been amused at the time, and it was clear that the affair still rankled. That Gerard Sterne should be small enough to believe the tissue of lies that the boutique owner had dreamed up though, could not but hurt Jenny.

Well, at least I shan't have to think up excuses not to be given a lift home to Bath, she told herself now, because Gerard is just as keen to avoid my company as I am to avoid his. But this bracing thought, far from cheering her up, actually brought tears to her eyes. Oh dear, she really had thought that he liked her!

Irritably, she wiped her eyes with her palms and told herself that she was being an idiot. Gerard Sterne could not have liked her, not even a little bit, or he would not have believed all that rubbish. And anyway, he was a medic, dammit, and she did not want to get involved with doctors! Yet when, seconds later, she felt hands go over her eyes she felt a tiny stab of excitement. Could it be . . .?

'Guess who, Jenny?'

Irritably, Jenny wrenched the hands from her eyes and turned to face Pierre Mongresin.

'Don't be silly, Doctor. If I'd dropped a cup it would have been your fault. I've finished now, so let me pass, please, I want to see a patient.'

Pierre, laughing, caught her hands in a gentle clasp, then looked more closely at her and sobered.

'You've been crying, pretty Jenny. What's the matter? Who's broken the heart of my favourite nurse?'

'I haven't been crying,' Jenny said mendaciously, pulling away from him. 'I've got to get Bob practising on his crutches, Doctor, but if you want to give me a hand . . .'

'Certainly I'll help,' Dr Mongresin said, falling into step beside her as she hurried out of the kitchen and along the corridor. 'Jenny, are you still upset over the fracas with the dog? It was nothing, all nonsense, truly, and Mr Hopwood was very sorry that he'd upset you. I dare say Sterne jumped to conclusions as well, but there's no ill-feeling now, I'm sure.'

'It doesn't matter,' Jenny said as they turned into Bob Anderson's room. 'I was upset, no one likes to be thought ill of like that, but I'm over the worst.' She smiled at Bob, sitting in his chair near the window, the plastered leg elevated. 'Good afternoon! We've come to interrupt your studies and get you to exercise.'

'I wasn't working, actually,' Bob said rather guiltily. 'I was spying. Take a look out there.'

Dr Mongresin and Jenny peered down into the grounds below them. For a moment all Jenny could see were strangers, and then she saw the familiar silver car. It was a fine day and the roof was open and inside it she could see Mr Sterne, talking earnestly to his passenger. He had one hand resting on her silk-clad knee. It was, of course, Janice Quinton.

'So what?' Dr Mongresin said, spotting the couple just as Jenny did. 'Everyone knows that Janice has been out to catch Gerard and it looks as though she's done it at last. I believe she's moved into his mews cottage, which is a good deal more convenient than her own place, since she lives miles from here. Sevenoaks, I think she said.'

'Well, it looks as though she's caught him,' Bob said, turning away from the window. 'Mind you, most of the rumours I've heard have turned out to be absolute rubbish, so probably he's just giving her a lift back to Sevenoaks. What do you think, Jenny?'

'I don't care much, one way or the other,' Jenny said airily, picking up Bob's crutches and holding them out to him. 'Neither of them are married so they can please themselves who they go out with. Now, just you concentrate on getting a good, even pace with these crutches, young man!'

CHAPTER FIVE

'MORE potatoes, Jenny?'

Jenny, Sandra and Stan Fox were sitting around the dining-table in the Fox's flat, eating the excellent dinner that Sandra had prepared. She had part-roasted the chicken and potatoes before leaving for work that morning, she informed her friend, and then when they got back after work she simply put the oven on again for thirty minutes and lit the gas under the vegetables, so that the cooking could continue quietly while she and her husband and their guest had a pre-dinner drink or two.

'More? I shouldn't, but I'd love one,' Jenny said, holding out her plate so that Sandra could spoon another richly browned potato on to it. 'You're a marvel, Sandra, to serve a meal like this when you've been working all day. You're very lucky, Stan!'

'Yes, she's a good cook, and a good hostess too,' Stan admitted. 'But she works too hard, like everyone else at the Royal. I wanted to take you both out for a meal tonight, but she wouldn't hear of it.'

'Jenny can have a meal out any time, but my cooking is something rare and valuable,' Sandra said, smiling at them both. 'What a miracle that everything got cooked when it should have done! You've no idea the mistakes I made when we first got married, but Stan smiled through them all. Undercooked fish, hard potatoes, rice pudding which was stiff as a board, melty jellies . . . You name it, I provided it! But I've improved a bit since then. Go on, Stan, have another potato and keep Jenny company.'

'Stop fishing for compliments, you *know* you're a cracking good cook,' Stan said, holding out his plate. 'I feel a bit mean since I can't help with the washing-up tonight, but I've got to get some work done.'

'That's all right. I enjoy wiping up and it's the least I can do to thank Sandra for a smashing meal,' Jenny assured him. 'Where do you study, Stan? Does poor Sandra have to creep around being terribly quiet, or is there somewhere far from the madding television where you can concentrate on your work without being disturbed?'

'Well, sometimes I work in the living-room and Sandra reads, or writes letters,' Stan said. 'But since you're here I'll pop back to the hospital and work there. I'll come back in time to run you home, of course.'

Jenny, smiling and attacking her pudding, thought with some dismay that she had guessed something of the sort. A glance at the duty rota had been sufficient to tell her that Dr Moran was on call tonight. She guessed that Stan would rush back to the hospital as soon as he could so as to dance attendance on the glamorous ophthalmic surgeon.

However, she could scarcely tell her host that she had guessed what he meant to do, so she continued to eat, wondering whether what she intended to do was for the best, or whether she was merely being very interfering. Because she had intended, when she accepted Sandra's invitation, to see whether she could warn Sandra, somehow, about Stan and Liza Moran, and now she believed she could do it without telling tales. Drying the dishes as Sandra washed them, she saw how it should be done.

'Does Stan often study at the hospital in the evenings?' she said casually, wiping the suds off an oval dinner plate. 'I shouldn't have thought a hospital was the ideal place for peace and quiet, even at night.'

'Yes, for the past two or three months he's been going back,' Sandra said, putting another plate into the drying rack. 'He sits in Mr Rodway's room and nips out when he hears the nurses making coffee in the ward kitchen and begs a cup. Sometimes I'm fast asleep in bed by the time he gets back here. But I mustn't grumble, I expect it's easier to study there.'

'Yet he hasn't been doing it all that long, so he's only recently discovered that it's easier,' Jenny said thoughtfully. 'I wonder why? I mean, I wonder what made him go to the hospital in the first place?'

'He began to get very impatient with me. Even if I turned a page noisily he'd snap, and then he got terribly fidgety, kept getting up and going through to the kitchen, or just peering out between the curtains, until I offered to go out myself for a few hours, give him complete peace. It was after that, I think, that it occurred to him that he could go back to the hospital. Of course, he'll study here for five or six days at a stretch sometimes, without any fuss, but then he'll get restless again.'

I bet he does, Jenny thought grimly. Every time he knows Liza Moran is on call. Aloud, she began to put her plan into operation.

'Gracious, that reminds me, I'll have to go back to the hospital before I go home tonight. Remember me getting Kat's suede suit out of the cleaners? I left it in the office, and I did mean to pick it up before I came away but I clean forgot. I'll just pop back, I think, and fetch it. Kat may easily need it tomorrow evening if she's going out.'

'We'll tell Stan when he calls for you,' Sandra began, but Jenny shook her head.

'No, that's silly, why should he make a double trip? My place isn't far from the Royal, so I suggest we take our time and walk over there. It's a lovely evening so it will be no hardship. It'll give me time to grab the parcel and to have a quick cup of coffee with Sister Lucas. She's good fun but we meet so rarely when we're on different shifts.'

'Oh. Go to the hospital when Stan's studying, you mean? Well, I could, but I don't want to annoy him, make him think I'm interrupting his work,' Sandra said uncertainly. 'He can be so very impatient when he's trying to study.'

'But he won't be working, he'll be thinking of packing up if we arrive about twenty past ten,' Jenny pointed out. 'He said he'd be back here to take me home by ten-thirty, so that will be just right. And think what fun it will be to surprise him!'

'Yes, that's true. We never go out now, you know, not with the exam so close. Yes, we'll do that. It will be quite romantic sharing coffee in Mr Rodway's room—or more romantic than being here alone,' Sandra said. 'Shall we watch TV for a bit? There's a play on later I rather wanted to see.'

The two girls had a pleasant evening and ten o'clock saw them putting light jackets over their dresses and setting off towards the Royal. Jenny rattled on about her life in Bath, modelling and nursing and she noticed with a slight stab of conscience that Sandra was rather quiet. What would her friend do if she found Stan and the wretched Liza in a compromising position? But I must be like a surgeon and hurt her for her own sake, she thought, as they trotted up the steps which led into the reception hall. In the end it will be best, I am sure of it.

'Here we are again,' Jenny said, stopping at the foot of the stairs. 'You go off to Stan in ENT, love, and I'll tackle Sister. Thanks for a really good evening, I think you're a smashing housewife.'

'Oh no you don't! Stan will be most upset if I let you walk home, even if it *is* only a step,' Sandra said firmly. 'He meant to leave at ten-thirty anyway, so suppose I give you a ring on the ward then? All you'll have to do is tear yourself away from Sister Lucas and run down to the car park, and Sir Stan will have you home in a brace of shakes—and without running any gauntlets, either!' Sandra knew all about the flat and the amusement arcade.

'Well, if you're sure . . .'

The two girls parted company and Jenny went up the stairs and into the office, where she was greeted with great warmth by Sister Lucas, who was brewing coffee in an electric percolator and cordially insisted on pouring Jenny a cup.

'And I've got some really good shortbread,' she said, opening a small red tin. 'Come on, Staff, just a tiny piece!'

In the end, Jenny spent half an hour with Sister, wondering all the while, with an increasing sense of guilt, what Sandra was doing. But at last the telephone bell rang and Sister picked it up.

'Sister Lucas, Annabel Goodson Ward,' she said. 'Oh, hallo, Sandra. Yes, she's here, we've just had a cuppa. To meet you in the foyer in two minutes? She's drunk her coffee, as it happens and picked up her parcel and I was just . . .' She stopped short, then put the receiver down, looking rather put out. 'There! Cut off,

I suppose. Still, you'll have gathered the gist of it. Nice seeing you, Staff.'

Jenny hurried down to the foyer, feeling thoroughly worried and still half wishing that she had not put her spoke in. Poor Sandra! Suppose . . .

But here was the hallway and there was her friend. She appeared to be studying a list of the hospital cricket team's future fixtures.

'Here I am, Sandra. I've got the suit.' She touched her friend's shoulder. 'Where's Stan?'

Sandra turned. Her face was pale and there was a hint of desperation in her dark eyes, but she spoke calmly enough.

'He's in the car park. Look, Jenny, shall we walk down there? He would bring the car round, but we might as well.'

Jenny waited until they were outside the hospital and heading for the car park and then stopped beneath a lamp standard and gazed searchingly at Sandra.

'What's upset you, Sandy? I'm not stupid, you know.'

'No, but I have been, haven't I?' Sandra heaved a tremulous sigh. 'Believing all the rubbish that Stan trotted out about working late and taking his studying back to the hospital for peace and quiet. I never even saw the danger when we stopped going out or having the odd meal away from the flat. It never even struck me that we were still just as hard up! What's worse, I took myself off to the cinema so that he could study in peace, or round to a friend's house . . . God, if I thought he'd been bringing that woman back to our flat . . . But he wouldn't go that far.' She swung round, away from the car park, and began to walk so briskly that Jenny had to trot to catch up. 'The swine! Well, he's just discovered that he didn't marry a doormat after all, so

I might as well tell you everything. I've left him.'

'You've *left* him?' Jenny could hardly believe her ears. 'Oh, Sandra, you can't mean it! Of course I've heard gossip which I bet never reached you, but . . .'

'I walked into Rodway's office and there was my husband, with his shirt unbuttoned, making love to some woman with long hair and lace underwear,' Sandra said with controlled violence. 'Or perhaps it would be more accurate to say she was making love to him! So I caught hold of her by that beautiful long hair and dragged her off him and gave her the sort of slapping she never had as a child, and told Stan I'd see him in court.'

'You didn't! Crumbs! What did he say?'

'Oh, what they always say, I believe. A moment's madness, it meant nothing, it would never happen again and all that. And the woman was crying and saying it was all a mistake and I couldn't really love him if I was prepared to ruin his reputation . . . Stuff like that. It was all terribly traumatic and dramatic and at the time I shook like a leaf—but do you know, Jenny, in a way it's like a heavy weight rolling off my shoulders, just to *know*? I knew something was the matter but I didn't know what, and I blamed myself.' She chuckled grimly. 'Not any more I don't!'

'I think you've done marvellously,' Jenny said. 'Then you don't think either one is really yearning for the other?'

'Not them! Poor Stan bit off more than he could chew. He'd want the kudos of having attracted a woman like her but he wouldn't expect to be set on physically.' She gave a small giggle. 'When I walked in he looked so appalled, Jenny, and that was before he'd registered that they had company! He's weak, I suppose, because he craves attention and admiration, but what he wants more than anything is stability and . . . well, and me. He really loves me, I know it now, even if I doubted it before. She was just something to boast about, to tell himself fantasies about. I expect he invented lots of lovely scenes where she vowed her undying love and sailed off into the sunset.'

'Well, spend the night with us and then forgive him tomorrow,' Jenny said practically, heartened to find that her friend was taking the whole affair so calmly. 'His exams are in a month, so you'll want to sort things out in plenty of time for that.'

They reached the flat, which was in darkness since Helen was working nights and the other two were both out, and once in the brightly lit kitchen Jenny put the kettle on and made two cups of coffee, glancing quickly at Sandra's white, strained face. Poor Sandra. She was a good deal more cut up than she pretended, but it would all be for the best. Jenny believed it even more now than she had done earlier.

Over the coffee, they discussed Liza Moran and Jenny told Sandra that Liza was, in fact, the ophthalmic registrar.

'She isn't a nice person, according to gossip,' Jenny said. 'But she is glamorous and they say most of the men are in full cry after her, so I expect Stan thought it was a feather in his cap to get her attention.'

'I suppose so,' Sandra said rather drearily. 'I've always known, of course, that marrying someone as handsome and attractive as Stan might bring certain difficulties, but somehow you believe that once you're his wife you'll be able to satisfy him. Anyway, it's best out in the open.'

'I think you're right. It will teach him to value you,

Sandra, and it will teach Liza Moran to keep her clutching little claws off other women's men!'

'You're right and I know it,' Sandra said, and a few minutes later the two of them made their way to bed, Sandra sleeping on a camp-bed in Jenny's room. But much later, when Jenny woke briefly, she heard her friend weeping into her pillow.

In the end, Sandra stayed at the flat for three nights before finally allowing Stan to persuade her to return home.

'I've only given in now because of the exams,' Sandra confided to Jenny as the two of them laid up the drugs trolley. 'Poor darling, I feel sorry for him, and I don't want him to fail just because of nervous tension. He's not eating properly either, and he's dreadfully pale. His clothes look as though he's slept in them, too.'

'He needs you, in other words,' Jenny observed. 'And you'll have heard that Liza Moran avoids him like the plague and goes around with her hair loose?'

'I knew they were avoiding each other but I don't know what her hair has got to do with it,' Sandra said, her hands coming to a halt over the neatly laid out display of capsules she had been counting. 'I haven't seen her myself.'

'You scratched her cheek when you slapped her and she's trying to hide it by wearing her hair brushed forward. Not that anyone's fooled for a moment. Person after person has said it'll teach her to leave married men alone, and there isn't anyone who doesn't admire the way you treated the whole thing.'

'Yes there is; Stan thinks I'm hard as nails.' Sandra permitted herself a small grin. 'However, when he picks me up from work tonight and we get back to the flat

I'm going to prove that I'm not a bit hard, but just his own loving wife.'

'Don't give in too completely,' Jenny advised. 'Remember, you'll be watching his every move for the next twenty years. That'll keep him on the straight and narrow.'

Later in the morning, as she hurried about her work, she met Bob Anderson in the corridor and admired his increasing confidence with the crutches.

'You'll soon be home,' she said as he swung to a halt beside her. 'And you aren't the only one.' Bob knew all about Sandra's stay with Jenny and her friends.

'She's going back? Good for her,' Bob said. 'I'm glad you admire my competence with these crutches because this afternoon I'm going to take a walk outside in the grounds. I'll go down in the lift, of course. Don't look accusing, Sterne said I could have a go! Nurse Black is going to come with me.'

'That's good. Where are you off to now, then?'

Bob grinned and gestured further up the corridor with his crutch.

'I'm going to get into the good books of the tonsillectomy.'

Jenny groaned. The tonsillectomy was a tough little boy called Norman Pyke and he was the despair of all the nursing staff. But he had a glamorous and delightful mother, a divorcee in her late twenties, Jenny supposed, and Mrs Pyke had taken to popping in at all hours of the day, usually clad in diaphanous summer dresses with low neck-lines. This fact, and her undoubted charm and flirtatiousness, meant that the susceptible veterinary student was even willing to put up with Norman for the sake of a few moments in her company.

'She's too old for you,' Jenny warned only half-jokingly. 'As for Norman, imagine being his step-father—He isn't the most accommodating child I know! And don't forget you're supposed to be working for those examinations.'

Bob opened his eyes very wide and looked righteous.

'I am working, that's why I spend so much time with Norman,' he protested. 'You don't think that kid's human, do you? Why, half an hour in his company and I know enough about the psychology of the great apes to get a job as keeper at London Zoo.'

'I know just what you mean,' Jenny groaned. She had spent her lunch-hour the previous day building a Lego robot for the young sufferer, to find, on completing the mammoth task, that Norman only wanted a robot so that he could blast it into a thousand pieces with an imaginary ray-gun and a very real fist.

Bob continued his journey up the corridor and Jenny went thoughtfully in to see her next patient. As she was working though, her mind kept returning to a painful fact. Gerard Sterne had been to see Bob Anderson and had told the lad that he could try his crutches out in the garden. But she had not known. A week earlier he would have informed her as a matter of course, knowing that she was interested in Bob's progress. But of course she had been avoiding him, finding excuses for leaving the room when she encountered him doing a ward round. It could not go on. She would have to face up to the fact that they must work together, even if they were at odds.

The next afternoon, when two patients had been returned from theatre and the ward was at its busiest, Jenny sustained her first real face-to-face encounter with Mr Sterne. Determined that she would not duck meetings with him, she would have remained in her patient's room at any rate, but as it happened she could not have escaped anyway, since the surgeon chose to arrive on the ward as Jenny was getting a patient back into bed after his operation.

The patient, a Mr James Selcott, was a diabetic. Peripheral vascular disease had meant that the amputation of a leg from the knee down had become essential. Jenny, having known in advance of the operation, was standing by, the bed already warmed. She knew Mr Selcott would be on blood with the cannula already in the vein, so the infusion stand stood ready. She checked over her equipment; cradle to protect the limb from the bedclothes, sandbags and a towel to immobilise the stump, mouth-wash and the equipment needed for observation on the trolley in the corner. When the door swung open and the patient was wheeled in she was ready, helping the porter and the nurse who had accompanied the patient up from theatre to lift Mr Selcott gently so that he was correctly positioned for easy nursing.

Even as she stood in the doorway seeing the porter and his trolley out, Gerard Sterne approached, slowed, and entered the room. He was still in his theatre gown and held a check-list in one hand. He spoke in his usual deep, firm voice, sounding neither embarrassed nor pleased over the encounter.

'Ah, Staff, you know this patient is a diabetic?'

'Yes, sir,' Jenny said quietly. She had the bedclothes rolled back and was arranging the sandbags on either side of the stump, with the towel over it and with the ends beneath the sandbags so that it would be held still and steady. Beneath his gaze, she adjusted the cradle and then pulled the bedclothes up, positioning them so that she would still be able to watch the stump.

'Good. He'll be wanting intensive nursing, I'm afraid. Are you to be in charge of him?'

'Yes, sir.'

He waited, as if he expected her to say something further, then nodded.

'Right. He'll want an injection for pain when he comes round. Make sure it's given and remember to watch that drainage tube; the drain needs emptying every six hours and he'll be on blood for forty-eight at the least. After that I'll probably want him on an intravenous drip.' He walked over and inspected the chart, which was still not filled in since Mr Selcott had only been back in bed a matter of minutes. With his back to her, he said, 'Flow all right? No trouble there?'

'Yes, sir.'

The temptation to snap that he had eyes in his head and that he had only to use them to see for himself that the blood was flowing normally was not difficult to resist. He was being so calm and practical, so damned impersonal! Oh, if only . . . Jenny found herself thinking, not for the first time, and hastily banished the thought.

'Good.'

He moved round and stood beside the patient's locker, drumming his fingers on the top and watching her as she moved about the room. Finally he broke the silence.

'Ever nursed an amputee before?'

'No, sir.'

She kept her eyes down, concentrating on her work, then moved round the bed and took down the chart. She might as well take Mr Selcott's pulse and bring the sphyg round so that she could check his blood pressure as soon as he awoke, but the consultant was between her and her patient. She was forced, for the first time, to meet his eyes.

'Excuse me, Mr Sterne. I can't reach my patient while you stand there.'

He was smiling. Not much, not as though he was very amused, but there was a definite softening of his hitherto detached expression. Jenny waited for him to mention their misunderstanding, perhaps even to apologise, but he merely continued to look down at her with a quizzical half-smile on his face.

'I'm sorry, Staff.' He moved aside. 'But I'm so happy to know that you're capable of uttering words other than a yes or a no.'

Jenny took Mr Selcott's wrist and, with her other hand, raised her fob watch. She kept her eyes steady on its small face, not deigning to glance at the surgeon.

Gerard Sterne was watching her, she knew that, and now he sighed. 'Nothing to say, Staff? I seem to remember you were rather a talkative young woman, before.'

'I'd rather not say anything which might be misconstrued, sir,' Jenny said quietly. 'It seems that you and I speak a different language in some respects.'

She could almost feel the frost forming in the air, but if he had expected to get back on reasonably good terms without retracting his statement that she was a liar, he had another think coming! Jenny put Mr Selcott's wrist down on the bedding and entered his pulse rate on the chart.

'If you expect me to apologise for speaking the truth, Staff, I'm afraid you don't know me very well,' Gerard Sterne said coldly, after a long pause. 'Naturally, I take into account the fact that Mr Hopwood had threatened to get you suspended and I know you love your work, so you invented a fictitious story which would save you from taking responsibility. I'm prepared to accept that you meant no harm and made a mistake.'

'And Sister? You aren't suggesting that she lied too? If so, don't you think she was taking rather a chance for a nurse she had only known a couple of weeks? Sir?'

She risked a glance at him. He was staring at the patient, a frown creasing his forehead.

'If you remember, Nurse, Sister did say it was *you* who had told her I'd agreed to the dog's visit. Can't we say that you were both mistaken and let it go at that?'

'Of course, sir,' Jenny said. Her hands were shaking as she pulled the trolley nearer the bed. She knew very well who was mistaken and who was not, but it was plainly useless to continue the discussion. Mr Sterne could not admit that there was even a possibility that he was in the wrong, so she might as well get used to the idea that she was branded as, if not a liar, an inventor. But it was no use trying to keep up a vendetta against a surgeon. He had far too much power.

After all, given that he had completely forgotten her request, it was equally possible that she, in her turn, might have forgotten to mention it and yet might think quite honestly that she had done so! It would be simple enough to be quiet, very polite and very formal—if only he could have brought himself to say he was sure she was not the liar he had as good as called her.

Wrapping the cuff round Mr Selcott's arm, she smiled as the patient's lids flickered upwards.

'Just taking your blood pressure, sir,' she said softly. 'How do you feel? I'll give you a mouth-wash in a moment, if you'd like that.'

He nodded feebly and Jenny began to pump. Behind her, Gerard Sterne cleared his throat.

'Nurse, perhaps it would be best if . . . damn it, Jenny . . .'

The door, opening behind him, cut the sentence off short. He muttered something which could have been a curse beneath his breath and then spoke normally.

'Ah, Sister, come to keep an eye on Staff? I think she's coping quite well, but this is her first amputee so I'd rather she wasn't left alone for too long.'

He left the room on the words, shutting the door firmly behind him. Sandra raised her brows at Jenny.

'All right? I saw him come in and I rather hoped he'd remembered and you were making it up. But when I came in the atmosphere was still a trifle chilly.'

'He's a man, and men never make mistakes,' Jenny said acidly. 'However, he amended his original statement, allowing me credit for being afraid that Hopwood would have me suspended. He almost gave in, mind you, when he suggested we might both be mistaken, only I could tell his heart wasn't in it. And what's worse, he refused point blank to take back the word "liar", so I must believe he still thinks it's true, allowing for a quibble or two about inventing.'

'Never mind, love. In my experience things like that have a way of sorting themselves out,' Sandra said. 'Finished doing the observation, have you?' She smiled at Mr Selcott. 'Right then, I'll take over here and give Mr Selcott a mouth-wash while you, Jenny, grab a cup of tea.'

CHAPTER SIX

'JENNY, say you will! Look, I'm not trying to compromise you or to swear undying love, all I'm asking is that you come with me to this sculpture exhibition and then for a meal afterwards. All above board, just for the pleasure of your company. Ah, be a sport!'

Pierre Mongresin's lively and expressive face was conveying pleading even better than his husky, accented voice. Jenny, leaning against the table in the middle of the sluice while the steriliser went through its routine, smiled at him. It was ages since she had been out for an evening with an attractive man, why should she not go? She had been getting on very well with Pierre, who had stoutly taken her side in the argument with Gerard Sterne, so why not go out with him? But she wanted to know more about the proposed evening, first.

'But Pierre, why sculpture, for goodness' sake? I don't know the first thing about it, I warn you.'

'Well nor do I, but I have to go because my cousin, Gessienne St Germain, is exhibiting and I have to write back to *mon oncle, ma tante,* and of course my own parents, to tell them how well she has done, how usefully she employs herself. But to go alone to such a place, to pretend to a knowledge and an interest which, frankly I do not have, would be a torment. Gessienne is a good enough sort of girl, but she is my cousin. To spend the evening with her would scarcely thrill me, even if it were not for the horrible sculpture. But if you were with me, dear Jenny, how nice the evening could be.' He grinned engagingly.

'And this South Bank, where the exhibition is being held, is of all places the least romantic. You will be as safe as houses, not so much as a dark corner will loom up, I assure you. And if it did, I would not take advantage of it. There! Now does that not sound a charming evening?'

Despite herself, Jenny laughed. Though Pierre would probably turn out to be as opportunistic as most men, he was good fun and she could not help liking him.

'All right then, thank you very much, I'll probably enjoy the sculptures at least as much as you will. But why should we eat out? I mean, a meal in a candlelit restaurant is bound to be romantic and to have dark corners.'

'We will eat in the full glare of a pizzeria, if you wish it,' Pierre said. 'You shall choose the restaurant. And I will take you to your very door in a taxi and the driver shall escort you to your flat. Jenny, it shall be the evening of your dreams!'

Jenny tried to forget that the one ingredient of her dream-evening would be Pierre's absence and Gerard's presence, and gave in gracefully to his suggestion that they should meet at seven o'clock. Then, having arranged a rendezvous known to them both, she began to load her trolley with the now sterile bedpans.

'Right, it's a date,' she said as they left the sluice together and went down the corridor towards the rooms. She paused outside the first door and as she went towards it it opened and Gerard Sterne came out. He looked briefly and coldly at Jenny and then behind her, at Pierre.

'Ah, it's you, Mongresin! I've been talking to Mr Hopwood and he told me . . .'

Jenny slipped past the consultant into the room he had just left, whose red light proclaimed that Miss Hilda Matthews still wanted a bedpan. She wondered whether Mr Sterne had guessed that she and Dr Mongresin were friends and what he would say if he knew they were going out together this evening. It would be lovely if he was jealous, but it would not cross his mind, except possibly to think Pierre a susceptible fool. She sighed, then left Miss Matthews and pushed her trolley along to the next room. Pierre and Gerard Sterne were still talking five minutes later as she returned to Miss Matthews for the first bedpan, and as she passed them Pierre spoke.

'Until tomorrow, then, Jenny. Don't be late.'

Jenny saw the consultant's expression change from indifference to surprise and then to annoyance. Good, she thought defiantly. He may not be jealous but he does not at all like me going out with Dr Mongresin. She smiled affectionately at Pierre.

'As if I should—I'm looking forward to it so much!'

Then, before either man could speak again, she turned her trolley in through the open doorway before her, and work claimed her full attention once more.

'I'm a dream in coffee and cream,' Jenny announced that evening, walking into the kitchen where Helen, just awake, was toasting brown bread. Helen glanced across at her, then, ruefully, down at her own buxom, uniformed person. She took off her glasses, rubbed her eyes, and then tucked a stray mouse-coloured curl back behind her ear.

'I loathe nights. I'll be glad when I'm back on a day shift again! But though I hate to admit it, you look a million dollars. That is the skirt and jacket you picked up in the Nearly New shop, isn't it? What have you done to it, you clever creature?'

The little cream jacket had a mandarin-style neck and Jenny had knotted a coffee coloured silk scarf round her throat and a brown and gold belt round her trim waist. The cream linen skirt flared above coffee coloured high heeled shoes and Jenny's long hair was tied back with a chiffon scarf which exactly matched the shoes.

'Done to it? Oh, you mean the scarf and the belt. It just goes to show that a little mix and match goes a long way. Do you remember how dowdy it looked when I tried it on? Next time I advise you as to a good buy, you listen to me.'

'Yes, but what looks like a good buy on you looks fresh from the jumble stall on me,' Helen grumbled, not without truth. 'Mind you, the prettiest dress I've ever owned was one of your bargains—the green linen one which I didn't want to get. Remember?'

'Uh-huh, I remember all my brilliant ideas,' Jenny said with a conspicuous lack of modesty. 'I may not have much else, but I do know what looks good, and so I should when you think of all the experience I've had with people who really do know the world of fashion.' She twirled experimentally and watched the skirt bell out. 'Yes, I approve of this outfit. Where's Kat? And Mandy?'

'Kat's gone into her room to change; she's got a date with the new houseman on Men's Surgical. Mandy went to a party. She grabbed her chiffon skirt and your black and silver evening blouse, she knew you wouldn't mind, and went back to Nan's to change there.'

Kat, entering the kitchen in a swirl of talcum and a towel and nothing else, put an end to the discussion by pointing out that Helen's toast was burning. Once the ensuing screams had subsided, however, and Helen had bolted, hastily eating the remnants of the toast as she thundered down the stairs, Katrina turned to her friend.

'How nice you look, dear. Who is he?'

'Pierre Mongresin. Just a friendly look round a sculpture exhibition and then a meal,' Jenny said offhandedly. 'And you?'

'Dr Evans—Johnny Evans. The one with thinning hair and glasses and the beautiful smile. I know he isn't handsome or a great catch but he'll be a darned good doctor, one of these days. Where are you going, did you say?'

'Sculpture. And you?'

'Out to Kew. I think it'll be fun.'

Jenny, who had been fiddling with the cream-coloured shoulder-bag which she intended to carry, suddenly dropped it on the table and ruffled Katrina's hair.

'Nice Kat, never a word about Pierre being a doctor or me being off men! He's a decent chap really, Dr Mongresin, and I was so sick of my own company and of feeling that I wasn't quite as nice as I'd always believed that it suddenly didn't matter that he was a member of the medical profession. All I wanted was to be taken out and laughed at and talked to for a change.'

'Don't I know the feeling!' Katrina smiled at the younger girl. 'But you've let Sterne's stupidity get at you and you really shouldn't, love. We all know you never lie and we all know you'd be the last person to involve another person in a lie. You'll just have to tell yourself that Sterne doesn't matter. It'll be easier, of course, if you find Mongresin good company and amusing.'

'I know. And I'm jolly well going to give him every

encouragement to date me often, if I enjoy myself tonight. I refuse to become an embittered spinster just to please Gerard Sterne!'

Katrina laughed and headed for the door.

'Good for you—not that I can imagine you as any sort of spinster for long, let alone an embittered one. Have a good time, darling, and forget all about Sterne!'

Jenny, vowing to do just that, made her way to the meeting place to find Pierre waiting for her. It was a wild and wonderful evening with the sun sinking flamboyantly into a bed of pink and gold cloudlets, and Jenny agreed to take a taxi to the exhibition hall, though she assured Pierre that the tube train would have been just as quick.

'But this is a treat,' Pierre said, sitting beside her in the cab. 'Besides, the quicker we are there the quicker we can be out again.'

They got out of the cab on the South Bank, but the wind, rising to gale force as they climbed the ramp to enter the exhibition, played a mean trick. It grabbed at the long, silky tail of Jenny's hair, whisked it out straight, and then slid her scarf off and away, waltzing high in the sky and far from their reach.

'Oh glory,' Jenny gasped as her hair began to lash around, whipping painfully into her eyes. 'This is the end! Why on earth didn't I do it in a bun or a French pleat?' She captured it in one hand as they entered the hall and smiled at Pierre. 'I'm sorry, I expect I look a mess now.'

'No, you look delightful,' Pierre said earnestly. 'But when we go out again I will lend you a hanky—I have a clean one—and then you can tie it out of the way until you get home.' He stroked a hand down the abundance of her long, pale gold hair. 'It is too beautiful, really, to tuck under a cap.'

'Fine,' Jenny said. She glanced round the entrance hall. 'Should we buy a catalogue? Otherwise we might miss your cousin's effort.'

They bought a catalogue and began. Through the many halls they wandered, glancing at the exhibits and then at each other. It was not so bad when huge, deformed-looking heads and bodies in various materials were on display; then it was possible to assume that it was their own ignorance which caused them to find the exhibits uniformly hideous. But what was one to make of a tower of brand-new, galvanised buckets, placed one upon the other, until they disappeared from view through a hole in the ceiling? Or a collection of bottles, some full of a darkish liquid, others empty, which took up floor space and merited a title and an artist's name displayed beside it? Or old football boots, piled with seeming negligence into a heap on the floor, each one with rusty nails pushed through the empty eyelets?

'When do we find your cousin's work?' Jenny asked at last, having suffered the agony of keeping a straight face through two whole floors of some of the most pretentious and alarmingly amateurish efforts that she had ever dreamed of. 'I just hope, for your sake, that her efforts are a bit better than . . .'

She broke off as a young man wandered across their path. He had shoulder length, daffodil coloured hair, pale blue eyes and a sensitive face which was not toughened much by his sporting what looked like a four-day growth of anaemic-looking beard. Jenny waited until he was out of earshot and then completed the sentence.

'. . . better than the things we've seen so far. I say, Pierre, that chap looked like an exhibitor to me. We'd better not giggle, I'd hate to hurt his feelings.'

'Hah! I ask myself do they think we are children or mindless morons, to be taken in by such things? I also ask myself whether they earn more money than I do in a month, just by piling up rubbish, tearing paper, throwing paint at walls and pulling the bristles out of brooms. That is what I ask myself!'

Jenny could not help sharing this very French and practical point of view and suggested that Pierre might consider making a pyramid of all the tonsils and adenoids he had removed during his career and presenting it to the next exhibition. This idea pleased them both so much that they were animated and laughing as they climbed the stairs to the third—and, Jenny hoped, final—floor. They arrived at the next hall and when someone called his name Pierre turned enquiringly, still with a smile on his lips.

'Yes? Aha, Gessienne!'

A very tiny, very pretty girl in a sari came towards them. She had clusters of dark curls all over her head, slanting dark eyes and a very sweet smile. She had a cast mark painted in red and gold in the middle of her forehead and she wore long, dangly imitation emerald earrings, but despite the clothing, she managed to look very French.

'Pierre, you came, and brought your friend Jenny! I shall show you round myself, since few people bother to come right up here. What do you think of the standard of the displays?'

'Oh! Ah, er . . .' Pierre said, flummoxed. Jenny, with a little longer to prepare a reply whilst he stammered, cut in.

'Everything is immensely interesting but rather above our heads,' she said firmly. And then, her sense of humour getting the better of her, added, 'Especially the buckets.'

Gessienne sighed and raised her eyes to the ceiling. 'Those buckets! People cannot take seriously an artist . . . But I should say nothing against the work of others. Interesting, I imagine, is a good word. And now, see what you think of *my* exhibit.'

Perhaps it was because of the memories of galvanised buckets, laceless football boots and empty bottles, but Gessienne's contribution to art shone with a clearer light as a result of what had gone before.

She had made doves out of every possible material from milk-bottle tops to lumps of coal, and they were beautiful. Silver, gold, black, white, blue, green and mauve, her doves swooped and rested and almost cooed at the onlookers. Several people who had gone in bemused silence round the rest of the exhibition were staring at Gessienne's doves and actually talking quite animatedly and Pierre and Jenny were happy to do the same.

Jenny was so grateful for the doves, which had saved them the embarrassment of having to pretend an admiration they did not feel, that she was all for including Gessienne in the dinner which was to follow. But Pierre had no such intention.

'We are going out to dine in the West End, little cousin,' he said, when they had finished admiring and were once more in the entrance hall. 'But one of these days we must make up a foursome, go out for a day together, eh? What's your young man called?'

'He is called Francis. Frank, they say at college. Frank Tillett.'

'Hm. Another artist, is he?'

Gessienne permitted herself a small, demure smile

but her eyes slid sideways at Jenny and held unholy glee. Jenny smiled back. It was all too clear that Pierre had no wish to make up a foursome with any of the people who had had a hand in this exhibition, apart from his cousin.

'No, and he would not thank you to ask the question—you would not ask the question if you could see him! Frank is doing a course in accountancy; he is very clever.'

'Oh.' Pierre brightened visibly and gave Jenny a relieved glance. 'Then see how he feels about making up a foursome, Gessienne. We could have a day out together.'

Later, sitting in the restaurant which, after all, had been his own choice, he expanded his suggestion as they both examined the huge menu.

'Gessienne is a good girl and works very hard; I have promised my aunt to keep an eye on her, meet this fellow she talks about and so on. You liked her, I could tell, and she you, so why should we not go out one Sunday when we are all free, perhaps into the country for a day?'

He put his hand on the top of Jenny's menu and bent it down so that he could smile coaxingly at her over the top of it. 'Please, Jenny?'

'Perhaps,' Jenny said, returning his smile. 'I'm not going to order my own meal, Pierre, because the prices scare me stiff and anyway, you're a Frenchman and this is a French restaurant, so I'll be guided by you.'

'Very well. And before you find out anyway, I must admit that I've done a few favours for the *patron* here, who just happens to come from the same village in Brittany as my father, so the prices need not concern us.' He shook a finger at Jenny as she began to protest.

'No, no, I wouldn't dream of taking advantage of a friendship. It is just that Mr Cormeau charges me as he would charge his own staff. Now, if you are to be guided by me . . .'

It was a delicious meal, right from the onion soup in small, individual casserole dishes, lidded with steaming melted cheese, to the apple pancakes flamed in cognac. Jenny finished off the last mouthful of her crêpe, sipped the small cup of exceedingly good coffee, and addressed Pierre across the now empty table.

'That was an education, Pierre. I don't feel much like walking, though—are you on call tonight? If you are, I foresee a certain lethargy overtaking you in about an hour!'

Pierre shook his head, looking so alert and hopeful that Jenny suddenly realised he would now expect her to invite him to come up to the flat for a nightcap—and she had no intention of doing any such thing. Young men were taken home to the flat, but not by Jenny, since it was tacitly understood that one did not ask a fellow there unless one had reasonably permanent intentions. Jenny, flitting happily from man to man and always keeping her friendships cool and manageable, had no intention of allowing Pierre to come any further than the new block of flats in Byron Road!

'I'm glad. I wish I could ask you back for a drink, Pierre, but as usual the flat is full of girls washing their hair and so on. Still, we can compromise. If you'll walk me some of the way home I'll buy you a drink in The Green Man, the pub near the hospital. It's quite near our flat.'

'We'll take a taxi to your very door,' Pierre protested. 'Or, if you would prefer it, you can come back to my place for a nightcap? I have a bachelor flat, very small, but compact, you know, and you would be most welcome there.'

In the end though, Pierre took her as far as The Green Man in a taxi. They stopped off there for a drink, and then he walked her as far as the respectable block of flats in Byron Road, where he thanked her punctiliously for her company, gazed earnestly into her eyes, and then kissed her so lightly that she was almost insulted, though she had no intention of allowing him to do anything more amorous. Nevertheless, since she had expected to have to fight him off, it was a blow to her pride to find him so correct.

Breezing back into the flat, therefore, no later than eleven-thirty, she was able to inform the only stay-at-home that evening, Mandy, that she had enjoyed her evening out but that all the stories about Frenchmen and their passionate natures were false.

'Charming manners; kissed me as though I were his elderly great-aunt and went,' Jenny said, sinking into a chair and staring morosely at the flickering television set. 'I think I'll go out with him again.'

'Has he asked you?'

'Mm. To the cinema tomorrow evening. I said no.' Jenny stared at the screen for a moment and then jumped to her feet with an impatient exclamation. 'Are you watching this stuff? No? Good, then you won't mind if I turn it off.'

'All right. Carry on, if you want to talk,' Mandy said resignedly. 'I gather you're annoyed because he didn't pounce, only you've always said you hate being grabbed on a first date.'

'I do, I really do. But . . . when you wait for it and nothing happens you ask yourself if you're losing your touch!'

Mandy laughed and reached for the packet of biscuits beside her chair. She began to munch, speaking rather thickly through her mouthful.

'Not you, you've just met a wily one, that's all. And I bet you made sure the circumstances weren't very propitious for an advance, didn't you?'

'Yes, that's true,' Jenny said, perking up a little. 'But Pierre always contrives to give the impression that he's barely able to resist kissing you violently every time you pass him on the ward, so I did expect . . .'

'If you ask me, he just behaved like that to get you really interested. At the start you'd decided the date would be a one-off, I think I recall? Yet now you're determined to see him again, if only to find out what he does,' Mandy said triumphantly. 'You wouldn't risk the cinema, but you made it quite clear that you'd go out again, didn't you?'

'Well, blow me down, you're right!' Jenny stared, wide-eyed, at her friend. 'How come you know so much about Frenchmen, Nurse Beckwith?'

'It's not Frenchmen, it's human nature, and I know more about it than you do because I've been alive longer,' Mandy said, taking another biscuit. 'And now that Auntie has solved your problem for you, can we turn the telly back on?'

'Then you *will* come? Ah, Jenny, you won't regret it! Making up a foursome isn't committing yourself to anything very much, but you'll enjoy a day out, especially if the weather's fine.' Pierre did his best to look soulful. 'Us doctors work terribly hard, you know. The least you nurses can do is make sure we relax when we're not on call.'

It was two days after the visit to the sculpture exhibition and Dr Mongresin had cornered Jenny in the laundry room where she was collecting clean bedding for a new patient. He was smiling, persuasive, confident that she would not let him down now that he had arranged a whole day out for them, so that he and Frank Tillett could make sure that Gessienne saw the sights whilst she was in London.

'We-ell, I am off this Sunday and I can't go home since I'm working Saturday, and I adore the Zoo, so I think I shall enjoy myself,' Jenny said. 'But what about meals? I know we've had two or three fine days in a row but suppose it rains? Picnics can be doleful in the rain.'

'If it rains Gessienne invites us all to her studio,' Pierre said, looking rather smug. 'We shall go there anyway for a meal in the evening, since Gessienne insists. My cousin is a good cook as well as a sculptress, and she's going to do us a meal which she says will be irresistible. Thank heaven you're coming, dear Jenny. Imagine what it would be like for me otherwise, trying to be chaperon to two little love-birds!'

He looked so disgusted that Jenny laughed.

'All right, I'll come, I've said I will! But only if you'll let me provide the lunch, since Gessienne's wining and dining us in her studio.'

'Yes, yes! Bravo!' Pierre grabbed Jenny and her armful of sheets and kissed her enthusiastically on the cheek, then squeezed her hard and moved his mouth hopefully nearer hers, planting little kisses as he went. Jenny laughed, pushed against his chest, and was brought up short by a voice speaking right in her ear, or so it seemed.

'Staff, what are you doing! Why aren't you with Mr Selcott?'

Jenny spun round. Mr Sterne stood in the doorway, his eyes condemning her, his mouth tight. Jenny saw his glance flick dismissively over Pierre, then return to her face.

'Well? Not tongue-tied, surely?'

The sarcastic bite in his voice was enough to bring all Jenny's instincts of self-preservation to the fore. She stood back from Pierre and straightened the pile of sheets in her arms ostentatiously.

'I'm about to lay up three beds, sir. Instead of going for my coffee-break. Dr Mongresin knows we're short-handed, which is why he came through here instead of waiting to see me when I'm not working.'

'Who is with Mr Selcott, then?'

'Sister, sir. But as soon as I've done the beds I'm going back to help her to change the blood container. It needs two of us, as I dare say you may know.'

Out of the corner of her eye Jenny saw Pierre stiffen and knew he thought she had gone too far, but she was on her mettle now. Damn Mr Sterne's vindictiveness. He had no right to come in here, chasing her during her rightful coffee-break and intimating that she could have no existence unless it was beside his patient. But he seemed to have lost interest in her now, and turned his cold eyes on her companion.

'Right. Mongresin, I've spoken to Dr Hopwood and he agrees that you can take charge of Selcott's diabetes for me, make sure the insulin level stays steady and so on. God knows, it's impossible for surgeons to keep up to date with something as complex as diabetes—that's very much your speciality, so if you could . . .'

He had been moving out of the room as he spoke, giving Pierre Mongresin little choice but to follow him, though as the younger doctor turned up the corridor he glanced back at Jenny, winked, and then pulled a rude face and made a gesture at Mr Sterne's oblivious back-view. Jenny, winking back, felt half-guilty for joining Pierre in his dislike of the consultant, but just at the moment she did not have much time for Mr Sterne herself. She knew he would not have spoken to any other nurse as he had just spoken to her. He could not resist showing her plainly that he no longer either liked or trusted her.

With her arms full of sheets and her heart heavy, Jenny made her way towards the empty rooms.

CHAPTER SEVEN

'THE NUMBER'S right, it matches up with the doctor's prescription, and the expiry date's all right, so we'll start.'

Jenny and Sandra were helping to put a hysterectomy patient on to blood, since she had been returned from the theatre without it and had suddenly begun to haemorrhage. Jenny smiled warmly at the patient as Dr Mongresin tightened the cuff of the sphygmomanometer round her arm to extend the distal veins.

'Not long now, Mrs Robbyns, and you'll be fine! You won't feel a thing, either.'

Jenny watched Dr Mongresin insert the cannula, check that the blood was flowing freely and nod to Sandra to release the clamp and then to her to begin bandaging the limb lightly into position on the board.

'Everything all right, girls? Mrs Robbyns? No discomfort? Well, someone will be watching for your light, so if you feel anything is not quite as it should be, you just ring that bell. We'll leave you to rest now, but you won't be alone, since Nurse Black will be along as soon as she's . . . Ah, here she is.'

Gillian Black entered the room, smiled at Dr Mongresin and then at Mrs Robbyns.

'All done, sir? I'll stay with Mrs Robbyns for a while, then.'

'And I'd better get back to Mr Selcott,' Jenny said guiltily, as she and Sandra left the room, with Pierre just behind them. She turned to address the doctor. 'He

142

was fine this morning, though, wasn't he, Doctor? He gave us a fright the other day, but once the insulin had been adjusted he seemed his usual cheerful self.'

'Yes, he is very well,' Dr Mongresin said. 'Between the two of us, Sister, Mr Selcott can scarcely blink without the fact being registered!' He touched Jenny's shoulder as she turned towards Mr Selcott's room and began to open the door. 'See you soon, Nurse!'

Jenny smiled and then entered her patient's room. Mr Selcott was sitting up in bed with a jigsaw spread out on the light bed-table before him. He was studying the pieces through a pair of half-glasses, but when he saw Jenny he smiled and pushed the table back.'Miss Dracula herself, I see.' He chuckled comfortably. 'After my blood again, eh? It's a wonder I've got any left to blush with!'

'I wish I didn't have to take it,' Jenny said ruefully, stabbing his thumb with an inward wince and quickly taking the necessary sample. 'But it's better that I do and you remain fit and healthy—and cheeky! How's the jigsaw going?'

'Not bad. If you've done your worst I'll have my thumb back. I was right on the verge of finding the missing piece of sky when you came in.' He watched as Jenny swung his table across the bed once more. 'Aha, just goes to show you our minds are better for a bit of a rest! Before you came in I was searching everywhere for that crow, the one down by the water's edge, and now it's the first thing my eye lights on!' Frail fingers, white as milk, picked up the piece and fitted it deftly into place. 'Ah, *now* we're getting somewhere.'

'I'll go and fetch your elevenses and then show you how a jigsaw *should* be done,' Jenny boasted. 'Isn't it odd how one's fingers itch to interfere with someone

else's jigsaw? Only I do wish you'd chosen an easier
one. You've doubled the difficulty by having an
autumn scene with a lake in it, since every one of
those beautiful coloured leaves has an upside-down
twin in the water.'

Jenny was half-way to the door when Mr Selcott's
voice stopped her.

'I hear you're going to the Tower of London, then?'

'Me? The Tower? What have I done to deserve that?'

Mr Selcott chuckled. 'A good deal, I dare say, if we
did but know! Now you know very well I mean with my
nice young doctor.'

'Oh, yes, I'm going sight-seeing with Dr Mongresin
and his cousin and her boyfriend,' Jenny admitted.
'How on earth did you find out?'

'Ah, it's surprising how people don't realise we're not
just patients, we're listening, too,' Mr Selcott disclosed.
'Mr Sterne came in here to have a word and Dr Mongresin was having a word at the same time, and something was said . . . Dear me, what was it now? Oh yes,
I remember, Mr Sterne seemed to be warning that nice
young chap that you'd got good friends, and that Bath
wasn't that far off.' Bright, inquisitive eyes met hers.
'Yes, I got the impression that Mr Sterne was none too
keen on Dr Mongresin taking Nurse Speed to the Tower
of London!'

'Oh?' Jenny turned away from the door. This would
have to be investigated! 'Now why on earth should Mr
Sterne take any interest in my affairs?'

'He said you were only young and not half as experienced as you liked to make out. Dr Mongresin got
quite sarcastic and hot under the collar,' Mr Selcott
said. 'Interesting, it was. They acted like a pair of young
dogs prowling round the same bone.'

'Well, isn't that charming?' Jenny said, heading back for the door. 'I'm a bone now, am I? I'll get your tea and your special biscuits and you can tell me the rest while I finish your jigsaw for you.'

But it transpired that there was no rest. Mr Sterne and Dr Mongresin had left the room at that point, so any further remarks that they might have made had gone unheard by Mr Selcott.

'I thought it was friendly of him, quite fatherly,' the patient remarked, as the two of them pored over the jigsaw. 'Concerned, he was, that the young chap didn't go taking advantage.' He shook his head. 'Heard a good deal about Frenchmen, I have. Just you keep in brightly lit places, my dear, and don't let him take you anywhere lonely.'

'Mr Selcott, I'm surprised at you,' Jenny said reproachfully. 'I thought you liked Dr Mongresin!'

'I do! But liking a man doesn't blind me to his faults, and you know what these foreigners can be like. A decent girl can't be too careful and Mr Sterne feels responsible for his nurses.'

'Does he indeed?' Jenny muttered. 'Oh look, there *is* a difference in the reflected sky. It's a bit paler, don't you think? Here, stop trying to fit water into sky and try it the other way up and you'll see.'

'Hmm. Yes, you're right. You've got yourself into my good books despite your bossy ways when it comes to my blood. Now, love, take an old man's advice and don't let that Frenchie take you back to his place; all right?'

'Oh, Mr Selcott, you aren't an old man, you're in the prime of life! And Dr Mongresin isn't like that, honestly he isn't.'

Mr Selcott stared hard at Jenny's flushed and indignant countenance and then nodded slowly, as if to himself.

'Maybe you're right. Then you just enjoy your outing, Nurse.'

'Patients, patients, everywhere,' Jenny muttered to herself later that day. She had taken more samples over to the path lab, she had scolded the child with the hernia for getting out of bed and she had carried a seemingly never-ending stream of flowers and chocolates and good wishes to a politician having her nose remodelled, though she had let it be known that it was her appendix which had been giving trouble.

Now, she was manoeuvring the tea-trolley through the doorway to the double room, laden with the tea and the cucumber sandwiches which Miss Stott and Mrs Franklyn had each afternoon, though Mrs Franklyn had so scared Miss Stott with threats of heart-trouble, obesity and varicose veins if she did not cut down her sweet-intake, that Miss Stott no longer had her slice of cake at tea-time. Jenny knew it would not hurt the elderly lady to miss out on a few slices of cake, but nevertheless she felt sorry for Miss Stott. She knew poor Miss Stott adored sweet things and missed that cake sadly.

Not that she would be doing so for much longer, for Miss Stott was due to depart the following day. Accordingly, as a treat, Jenny had defiantly placed two noble slices of iced fruit cake on her trolley and she intended to share it between the two ladies.

'Good afternoon!' she greeted them as she entered the room. 'China tea for two, as ordered. And sandwiches. And a piece of cake each, to celebrate Miss

Stott's release tomorrow and Mrs Franklyn's release at the end of the week.'

'Ooh, iced cake,' Miss Stott said, her eyes glistening. 'Nurse, I do believe that just this once . . .'

Mrs Franklyn sniffed, then nodded. 'Yes, very well. Just this once I'll indulge. Shall I pour, dear?'

This last remark, addressed to Miss Stott, showed better than anything else what a hold Mrs Franklyn had gained over the staff, since other patients made do with a cup of tea and had no choice but to accept what was offered. Mrs Franklyn, however, had soon dispelled any hopes the staff might have nurtured of treating her like other patients.

'I abhor Indian tea or this unnamed blend that probably means it was brushed off some factory floor,' she had said briskly on her third day in hospital. 'I always have china tea, without milk, and brewed for no longer than five minutes. If you'll bring me a pot through, just a pot with boiling water in it, then I'll undertake to make tea just the way it should be made.'

Weakly, Jenny had taken the problem to Sandra and had watched with some amusement as Sister had tackled Mrs Franklyn with reason, firmness and logic, only to find them swept unceremoniously aside.

It was extravagant to provide china tea for one? But how much more extravagant to provide a cup of tea each day which would be wasted, poured down the drain, because it was undrinkable! And why should it take a nurse longer to pour boiling water into a small pot than it took her to pour it into a larger pot and thence into a cup? While she thought it a bad economy to buy blended tea because it was cheaper and easier to obtain, she did understand that large institutions found such so-called economies necessary, and therefore she

would not object to buying her own tea and keeping it
in a small tin in her room.

'I won't insist on lemon,' she had finished grandly.
'But decent tea I really must have. And as for your
apparent fear of a patients' revolt, how many other
patients have complained about the quality of the
tea?'

Sandra, backing out of the room, was heard to mutter
that if Mrs Franklyn really did not mind buying her own
tea . . . And thereafter Jenny bought the fine china tea,
took the boiling water through, and very quickly ended
up, as she had known she would, by making the tea in
the small pot since Mrs Franklyn quickly explained that
though she *knew* Jenny tried, the water was never quite
hot enough after its journey from the ward kitchen to
make really first-rate tea!

'Mrs Franklyn,' Jenny had said as she took charge of
the tea and carried it through to the kitchen, 'you are
like Chinese water-torture; you don't hit us over the
head to get what you want, you just keep dripping away
quietly until the first crack in our defences appears.'

'What an unpleasant simile,' Mrs Franklyn said dis-
approvingly, but there was a twinkle in her eye. 'However, if you mean that I've learned *softlee softlee catchee
monkee*, then I would agree with your diagnosis.'

So now, watching the tea ritual, Jenny wondered
whether Miss Stott really enjoyed the straw-coloured
brew; if she did not, she never complained. Poor Miss
Stott, she would regard her stay in hospital with very
mixed feelings, Jenny thought.

However, she was wrong. Miss Stott had enjoyed
every moment of it and was saying as much now, as the
tea streamed from the pot into the cup.

'. . . marvellous to see my dear Baby, but how I shall

miss my good friends,' she was saying rather tearfully as the door opened. 'Oh, it's Mr Sterne! I expect he'd like a cup of your delicious tea, my dear.'

The consultant, entering the room quickly, nearly cannoned into the trolley, apologised to it, gave Jenny. who giggled, a brief, unsmiling glance and then replied to Miss Stott with his customary courtesy.

'Tea? It certainly looks very good, but I won't, thank you, since Sister always has a cup ready for me when I've finished my round.'

Mrs Franklyn sniffed.

'A cup! Yes, my dear boy, some dreadful blend probably swept off some . . .'

'Factory floor,' Gerard Sterne finished for her. 'I'm afraid my jaded palate has grown accustomed to awful hospital tea and dreadful hospital coffee! But I've come in to say goodbye for now to Miss Stott, and to wish her continuing good health.' He smiled at Miss Stott, then at his old teacher. 'I expect you two will continue to meet from time to time?'

Both ladies assured him that this would be so, and Mrs Franklyn went on to give details.

'Indeed, we've become such good friends that we would not dream of letting the friendship lapse. When Miss Stott takes Baby for his walk she's going to pop in for a cup of tea, and then the next day I'll do my shopping and call on her at coffee-time.'

'Very nice,' Mr Sterne said approvingly. 'Incidentally, Miss Stott, did Baby come and visit you? I never saw him, I'm afraid.'

There was a startled silence before Mrs Franklyn answered for her friend.

'Indeed you did see Baby, Mr Sterne. And what was more you shouted at Nurse to get him out of our room!

You cannot have forgotten Baby. His size alone should make such a thing impossible.'

Mr Sterne stared, then swung round to Jenny, completely ignoring his two elderly patients.

'Nurse? You don't mean that monster was Baby? But a *dog* . . . I thought . . .'

'That's right,' Jenny said grimly. 'That monster was Baby. I'm glad your memory was eventually jogged.'

'Memory?' He swung round, catching her arm and taking her with him into the corridor. As he closed the door he said, 'Back in a minute, ladies,' and then he was hurrying Jenny towards the office. 'Come in here for a moment, young lady.'

Jenny, towed willy-nilly in his wake, felt lighter at heart than she had done for some time. The stupid man! He had just not believed the vast Alsatian could possibly be called Baby, and she had not realised that he had not realised. Thus did misunderstandings arise!

They reached the office, which was empty, and Mr Sterne sat her down in the visitor's chair and then took his own place behind the desk.

'Come on, Jenny, it looks as though we're going to get the matter cleared up at last. Tell me the whole story, not omitting the dog's name this time.'

'Right. I asked you if Baby could visit Miss Stott for half-an-hour or so. Naturally, I knew he was a dog, though I did think he was a tiny one from what she'd said. And you said yes, you know you did!'

'Of course, because I thought Baby was a neighbour's child or perhaps a great-nephew. As you know, we don't encourage children to visit the ordinary wards on a weekday, so I thought you were seeking my special permission for that reason. It never occurred to me for one moment that Baby might have four legs and not two. But you, of course, never actually used the word "dog" because you took it for granted that I knew Baby was Miss Stott's pet.' He stood up, his expression rueful, and held out a hand across the desk that separated them. 'I owe you an abject apology, Jenny. I'm very sorry I leapt to conclusions and misjudged you. There!'

'It's all right,' Jenny said flatly. She took his hand, shook it briefly and then faced him across the desk without smiling. She had no intention of letting Gerard Sterne's looks and machismo work any more damage on her once-susceptible heart. 'Would you mind explaining to Sister and Mr Hopwood, please?'

'Yes, of course.' He looked rather puzzled. 'I have apologised, Jenny, and I meant every word of it. I should have known you wouldn't tell even the mildest of lies. And I'm sure all the things that Douglas Whelpton said about you were spite.'

'I expect so, but I couldn't say since I don't know what they were,' Jenny said, her voice cooling several degrees. If he dared to insinuate that she had lied over Whelpton that really would finish him in her eyes!

'Well, he said you went willingly enough to Hastings, that you'd been out with him several times in fact. He insinuated that you'd been more than friends.'

'Did he? Well it happens to be untrue, though I did go out with him before I discovered what sort of a person he was. But it's really all rather beside the point, isn't it, sir? It happened a long time ago and it has nothing whatsoever to do with my nursing career here at the Royal.'

'That's true, but . . . Damn it, Jenny, you're not so very old, and if you let types like Whelpton take you out then what you need is a permanent keeper!' Mr Sterne got up and came round the desk, catching Jenny's hands in a warm clasp. 'My dear girl, you're far too trusting. I don't want to see you getting into deep water with some fellow who . . .'

Jenny wrenched her hands away and stepped backwards, feeling the heat rise in her cheeks. Was he insinuating that Pierre would take advantage of her in any way? If so . . .!

'I'm quite capable of taking care of myself thank you, sir; I've been doing it for years! And if you're trying to say that Dr Mongresin is not absolutely trustworthy, you can save your breath because you're quite wrong.'

'My dear girl, you've been out with the fellow once or twice and you think you know him! That just shows you're far too trusting, and I don't want it to end in tears.'

'Why not?'

Mr Sterne looked surprised and a trifle confused. No wonder, Jenny thought maliciously. He was behaving as though he was some sort of father-figure and he was very far from being that!

'Well, because I'm fond of you and . . . look, how about meeting me this evening after work? I'll take you out for a meal and we can talk this whole thing over.'

'No thank you.'

She saw astonishment flare in his eyes and felt considerable satisfaction. Let him know what it was like to be refused—and anyway, how could she possibly go out with him, when she knew very well that he was carrying on with the Quinton woman?

'No? But damn it, Jenny, we got on so well, I thought . . .'

'No, Mr Sterne. And now, since I'm on duty, I'm afraid I must go.'

She marched out of the office, her apron rustling and

her shoes squeaking a little on the polished lino. She felt outraged, all right, but a little sad, too, and sternly resisted a temptation to look back, to smile and encourage him to come after her, repeat his invitation. After all, hospital gossip was notorious. He might merely have been giving Janice a lift home. With his hand on her knee? Oh damn the man!

He did not follow her. As she swung into Room Six he was standing stock-still in the doorway of Sister's office.

At nine o'clock on Sunday morning, Jenny was in the kitchen, packing the picnic for her outing and feeling fairly satisfied with life. She and Mr Sterne could scarcely be said to be on good terms, but at least they were not at daggers drawn, as they had been before. And this time most of the annoyance was on her side. Because whatever he might think, he had no right to insinuate that she was not able to take care of herself, and even less to insinuate that Pierre would behave in anything other than a gentlemanly way. And from what she could gather, his affair with Janice Quinton was still on. Why should the consultant not take Janice out, indeed, since both were unmarried and fancy free? But he could scarcely expect Jenny to share his attentions with the other girl!

She sometimes played with the idea of his giving Janice up and asking her again, in a suitably humble way of course, to go out with him. What would she say then? But she knew that it would have to be a firm no once more. After all, she had no wish to get heavily involved and she had very nearly lost, if not her heart, then her head!

The previous evening Jenny had done some cooking,

determined to show Gessienne that an English girl could cook as well as a French one. Now she put a box with tiny Cornish pasties inside it into the lunch basket, then another box containing bite-sized sausage rolls and then a rich fruit cake wrapped in foil. There was a cold roast chicken, a lidded plastic bowl full of crisp salad, and a bag containing home-made bread rolls. Finally she fitted a number of luscious pears round the other food, and added a pat of butter, hard from the freeze-box of the fridge. That should do them very nicely, she thought approvingly. Pierre was providing wine and after the meal they would buy coffee just to round it all off.

Experimentally, Jenny hefted the basket. It was heavy, but by no means impossible, especially to a nurse used to lifting weights. In one of the bedrooms someone stirred and a sleep-drugged voice called out that she was to have a good time. Jenny, smiling, popped her head round Katrina's door, to see her friend's face emerge, tortoiselike, from the covers and grin.

'Sorry, I was trying to be very quiet. You need your sleep,' she murmured. 'I'll be back late, don't know what time. Fancy a cuppa? I've got twenty minutes before Pierre arrives.'

'I wouldn't mind. You look nice and cool.'

'Yes, it's going to be a scorcher, I think. I'll get the tea.'

Jenny was wearing blue matelot pants and a white halter top and her hair was tied back in a pony-tail. She looked neat rather than glamorous, but it was to be a practical sort of day, with a visit to the Tower first and then, because they wanted to take advantage of the glorious weather, a trip to the Zoo. Pierre was meeting her outside the new flats at nine-thirty, so she made the tea, took a cup through to Katrina, drank her own, and then set out, the basket swinging at her side and a blue silk jacket threaded through the handles in case it got chilly later.

Pierre arrived at the meeting place just as she did, driving a blue Ford with a sun-roof, open at the moment. He grinned at her and leaned across to open the door.

'How nice you look, and right on time, too! Hop in, and you can rustle Gessienne up while I wait in the car.'

Jenny got in and put her picnic basket on the back seat, then turned to Pierre.

'Where does Gessienne live? Somewhere very arty, I dare say.'

'I don't know about that, but it's awkward, as you'll see when we get there. If she isn't waiting, and I bet she won't be, then if you wouldn't mind fetching her I'd be obliged.'

Gessienne, it transpired, had a flat above a grocer's shop and a thriving Sunday market was being held the length and breadth of her street. It would have been impossible for Pierre to have left the car since the roadway was clogged with people and stalls, but there was no sign of his cousin.

'I'll drop you off and then drive slowly round the block and be back here in five minutes,' Pierre said resignedly. 'Do try to get Gessienne moving, there's a love.'

'Yes, I'll do my best.'

Jenny hopped out of the car and rang the bell outside the shop. There was a short silence and then a breathy and distorted voice said, right in her ear, 'Is that Jenny?'

Jenny looked round, and saw an entryphone above the bell. 'Yes, it's me,' she said. 'Are you ready, Gessienne?'

'Nearly. Here, I've unlocked. Come on up.'

Jenny heard the click and went through the door, up the stairs, and into the flat. It appeared to consist of the studio itself, a huge, bare room, a tiny kitchen and nothing else, though Gessienne informed her that the bathroom was shared and on the ground floor.

'I shan't be a minute, Jenny,' she said, taking in the other girl's appearance with interest. 'Is that what I should wear, today? Not my sari, no?'

'I don't think it matters,' Jenny said soothingly. 'Is a sari cool enough for a day like this? It's really hot outside.'

'Yes, but if you wear trouser, so do I.'

Gessienne had been standing in the middle of the studio in a dark red silk sari, but now she slipped out of it and walked across the room to a built-in cupboard containing a great many very colourful looking clothes. She selected a pair of rose-pink silk trousers and a baggy white top and put them on, then turned to Jenny once more.

'All right? I have no short trousers, like yours, but these are very cool, very comfortable.'

'Fine. Will you take a jacket in case it gets cooler later? I've left mine in the car.'

Gessienne bit her lip, thought, then shook her head.

'No, it won't be necessary since we come back here to dine and I shall not be going out again. Come, then.'

They rejoined Pierre in the car just as he was coming round for the second time, and picked up Frank Tillett without any problems since he was already waiting for them on the edge of the pavement. He was very different from Gessienne, a fair-haired young man with a rather serious outlook on life, but he adored his vivacious little

girlfriend and became quite talkative once he got to
know Pierre and Jenny.

'Well, off we go,' Pierre remarked as he put the car
into gear and turned it towards the Tower. 'Let's make
this day memorable, my friends!'

'It has been the loveliest day and you are very kind,
cousin,' Gessienne murmured as the car drew up once
more near her flat. At this time of the evening the
Sunday market was clearing away, the stalls no longer
attracting customers, and it was possible for Pierre to
park his car right outside Gessienne's flat. Gessienne
and Frank, entangled amorously on the back seat,
straightened themselves out and prepared to alight as
Pierre parked neatly alongside the kerb and Jenny
hopped out, swinging the now empty picnic basket, and
waited for the other three near the flat.

'Now where is the key?' Gessienne muttered, searching the voluminous folds of her white blouse. 'There is
a pocket here somewhere, I know, and I put the key
. . . ah!' She withdrew the key and turned towards her
door. 'We will go first, Jenny, whilst Pierre locks his
baby up. Don't men fuss about cars? And then we can
get the meal started.'

Jenny, agreeing, glanced back towards the young
doctor, who was locking his car, and was about to face
front again and start up the stairs when she heard a
fracas break out behind her. Two of the stallholders
were arguing, shouting, and one of them stepped
towards Pierre. Could he be objecting to Pierre parking
the car at that precise spot? Would it, perhaps, get in
his way as he took down his stall?

They were destined never to know. At that moment
a fist was raised, an insult thrown, and before they could

do more than blink, a full-scale fight was taking place. One minute Pierre was straightening, turning away from his car, and the next he had disappeared from view as a flood of humanity engulfed him.

'Police! Get the police!' Jenny shouted, knowing from the amusement arcade that the mention of the word police made fighting men come to their senses. And on this occasion it did more than that, since two constables seemed almost to materialise on the pavement, wading in briskly, blowing whistles and seizing the combatants with surprising speed and effectiveness.

In less time than it takes to tell, the fight was over, the police were in control and men with blackened eyes or bruised shins were moving sheepishly away from the scene.

But not Pierre. He lay, half on the pavement and half in the roadway, ominously still.

CHAPTER EIGHT

'YOU COULD have knocked me down with a feather!' Sandra stared at Jenny across the desk. 'I walked into Room Three this morning when Sister Lucas told me to go and take a look at the emergency admission and there was Dr Mongresin, with the drip dripping away and a cradle over his leg, looking so pale and interesting that for a moment I didn't recognise him! And you brought him in, Sister said.'

Jenny, counting tablets, nodded and tightened the cap on the bottle.

'That's right. Just my luck that the poor chap had to get overtaken by a fight when we were about to have dinner with his cousin and her boyfriend. Anyway, we rang for an ambulance and I travelled back here with him in it, and I dare say you can guess the first person I saw.'

'Was it your friend Helen? She's on Casualty, isn't she? And on nights, too.'

'Well, she is, but actually it was Gerard Sterne. He wasn't the first person I saw either, how I do exaggerate! But as soon as the houseman realised it was a fissure of the patella, Sterne was sent for, since he was on call. I gave a hand to aspirate the swelling—it was up like a balloon by the time Mr Sterne arrived—and then I stayed until Pierre was in bed and fairly comfortable. Sterne injected a long-lasting local anaesthetic, so Pierre was asleep when I left. How is he this morning? Doctors are usually rotten patients, but that's a nasty fracture, and he's cracked a couple of ribs as well, so I expect he's quite content to be where he is for the time.'

'He ate some breakfast, though not very much. He isn't grumbling, but he's sleepy still. He's had pain-killers, of course, so he probably isn't fully aware yet. Anyway, if you're going to do the drug round you'll see for yourself.' Sandra laughed. 'Poor Jenny, your boyfriends go down like ninepins, don't they? First Sterne, then the bunion, now a horrid fracture!'

'He isn't my boyfriend,' Jenny said quickly. 'None of them were, not really. Give me the chart, would you, and I'll fetch Carew and get started.'

As Jenny and Nurse Carew greeted patients and dispensed drugs, Jenny thought about the disastrous end to her lovely day out. Pierre, groaning and bloodied from a kick in the face, being lifted tenderly into the ambulance, Gessienne crying, Frank blaming himself for not having realised in time that there was trouble brewing . . . And then, to cap it all, Gerard Sterne's words when he walked into the cubicle and saw her holding Pierre's hand.

'I see you've got the medical staff fighting over you now, Nurse,' he had said. 'Or did you kneecap Dr Mongresin in self-defence?'

Jenny had smiled frostily. No use to take offence at the look in his eyes, which was a sarcastic, told-you-so sort of look, when his tone reflected such determined joviality.

'Neither, sir. He was knocked down by a running fight that swept straight over him. I think the damage was done accidentally, by feet rather than fists.'

'Hmm. And where did this take place?'

'In a street market. Pierre parked his car and a fight started.'

'I see. Well, I'll put him on Annabel Goodson when I've tidied him up a bit. I expect you'll want to stay with him until he comes round.'

She had stayed. And now, entering Room Three, she put on her brightest smile. Last night he had clung to her hand, dry-lipped, gasping, until he had fallen asleep. He had been very lucky, for although he had been concussed from a blow to the skull, it was a superficial blow only, as X-rays had proved. Now she would have to reconcile him to a longish stay in bed.

'Hallo, Pierre! How do you feel? I'm afraid they won't let you get up yet, but in two or three days you'll be limping round with the help of a back-splint, crutches and a nurse or two. Ribs sore? And how's the face?'

Pierre, leaning against his pillows, was white still, and sleepy, too, but he smiled back at her.

'Not too bad, but I wish it hadn't happened. What an ending to a good day out, eh? And this will keep me away from work for two or three weeks.'

Or longer, Jenny said in her mind, but there was no point in telling Pierre what he already knew. He would come round to it in time, and anyway, once he was on crutches he could totter around the Annabel Goodson ward and check on his patients even though he would not be able to return to work proper for a while.

'Don't worry about it. Just be thankful it wasn't any worse,' she advised. 'I've got some capsules for you; we aspirated the knee and Mr Sterne decided you'd better have antibiotic.'

'Right. I'll take them with some water. Incidentally, the knee hurts like fun but I hope there's no question of separation?'

Jenny shook her head.

'No, Mr Sterne said it should unite given rest and no

exercise until he gives you the go-ahead. So just be sensible and you'll soon be on your feet again.'

'And when I am, you and I . . .' Pierre saw the open interest on little Nurse Carew's face and turned the words into a mumble. 'Come back and have your coffee-break with me, and then we can talk.'

'Yes, of course I will,' Jenny said, and smiled at Nurse Carew as they left the room and proceeded down the corridor. 'Poor Dr Mongresin, I'm afraid he'll be with us for a while yet.'

'It looks like it. Are you going out with Dr Mongresin, Staff? I thought someone said you were.'

'Not really, or only just on a friendly basis,' Jenny said. 'I was with him when he was injured, because I'd made up a foursome, but other than that . . .'

'You're just good friends, Staff?'

The two girls laughed together as they continued with their work.

'Never did a man have more visitors,' Jenny groaned to Katrina, as they sat opposite each other in the canteen at lunch-time. 'Pierre just lies there looking wan and interesting and every doctor and nurse in the hospital passes along the corridor going to cheer him up. I didn't realise he was so popular.'

'It isn't that, it's "there but for the grace of God go I," ' Katrina observed, spearing a piece of quiche on her fork and popping it into her mouth. 'How about Sterne? Does he dance attendance on his fellow medic?'

'He's around a lot,' Jenny admitted. 'Comes to see Mr Selcott two or three times a day and pops in on Pierre when he's on the ward. Those two don't really like each other, but that doesn't stop him being very conscientious about Pierre, I'll give him that. He's even given his work of looking after the diabetic side of Mr Selcott's illness to Dr Anwalla, though Pierre did offer to get me to act as intermediary.'

'That's much the best. He won't want you and Pierre to muck things up between you,' Katrina said callously. Anyway, didn't you say he disapproved of you going out with Pierre?'

'Oh, that! He seems to have forgotten it now, at any rate. Though he did make a nasty, sarky sort of remark about never knowing what he was going to find when he walked into Pierre's room.' Jenny snorted. 'As if he wouldn't have been surprised to find both of us in the wretched bed!'

'Serve you right for getting involved with the medical staff, after all you'd said,' Katrina observed cruelly. 'And if you give Pierre the elbow now it will look absolutely awful, with him so ill and poorly.'

'I know. Oh well, I'm off back to the slave-ring,' Jenny said, getting to her feet and carrying her dishes back to the kitchen hatch. 'See you tonight, Kat.'

Back on the ward, Jenny charged a Redivac drain, dealt with a drip that was not flowing properly because the top of the cannula was occluded by the wall of the vein and helped an elderly patient with a walking aid to manoeuvre himself and his equipment through the doorway of his bathroom and toilet. Then she went and took blood from the ever-patient Mr Selcott, told him cheerfully that Dr Anwalla would not be long and would introduce himself, and hurried off to join Mr Hopwood's ward round.

It was proving to be one of those days when nothing goes right. Pat Roach was away, Gillian Black had gone to the dentist's, and Nurse Carew was only a cadet and had to be watched all the time. The other girl, Nurse

Wellman, was in class this week, which meant that Sandra, Jenny and the cadet were managing somehow between them.

Sandra let the door swing back on the trolley when it had been laid up for dressings and several pieces of equipment were rendered unsterile. Nurse Carew forgot to put a rubber draw-sheet on a new patient's bed and then tripped and spilled tea everywhere, and Dr Mongresin told all and sundry that his head ached, his knee hurt, and he wanted company.

He tried to press Jenny into visiting him that evening and Jenny, tired out from having stayed with him at the hospital the previous night until the small hours, snapped crossly at him. He looked hurt and pouted like a small boy and Jenny, realising that he did not know the extent of her sacrifice since he had been unconscious for most of it, laughed and was actually sitting on his bed and smoothing his brow when the door opened to admit Mr Sterne.

'I'm sorry, Pierre, but when I'm tired I do tend to snap and get cross,' she was saying as the surgeon entered the room. She fell silent at once and stood up, but Mr Sterne did not intend to follow her example. His brows rose and his eyes gleamed menacingly.

'Ah, Nurse, having a rest, I see. Your devotion to Dr Mongresin is touching, but please don't forget you're in charge of Mr Selcott. How is he?'

'Fine, sir.' Red-faced, Jenny headed for the door. 'I'll leave you to see Dr Mongresin and I'll go and check Mr Selcott.'

Outside in the corridor she put hands up to her hot cheeks. Wouldn't you know it, she thought, Gerard Sterne was always around when she did not want him to be! She found herself longing for the evening to come, so that she could be away from the hospital for a few blissful hours. Having Dr Mongresin as a patient was proving far from easy!

'Hallo, Mandy, put the kettle on, there's a darling.'

Mandy grinned as Jenny and Katrina burst into the kitchen, then filled the kettle and put it on the stove as her two friends flopped into the chairs drawn up by the table.

'You look worn out, the pair of you. By the way Jenny, your agent phoned. Said were you free this Wednesday afternoon, so I looked at the calendar and told her after three, and she said that would be fine and would you ring her back?'

'Oh?' Jenny perked up a bit. The extra money would be lovely and for once she felt that it would be even nicer to relax, to put on beautiful clothes and just pose in them and not spend the time flying from pillar to post and getting scolded. 'What was it about? Did she say?'

'No. I said you'd ring after six, at home.'

Jenny duly rang after six, to find that Netta Bland, her agent, had provisionally booked her to do some work for Ralph Melville, a photographer she had frequently worked for. She agreed, made a date, and was then delighted and surprised to find that Ralph was also offering a trip to Paris for photographic work not too far in the future.

'That would be fine, but did he ask for me?' Jenny said, rather puzzled. Ralph had used her often in the old days, but lately he had not given her a lot of work and she had assumed that he did not much approve of her part-time attitude to the job. She had made it too plain that nursing must and would come first, willing though she was to model in her spare time.

'Yes, he particularly asked for you,' Netta assured her. 'They want a blonde, a leggy one.'

'Oh. How do I find out more about the Paris job then, Netta?'

'Ralph will fill you in on Wednesday afternoon. Bye, sweet.'

Next day the work continued fast and furious. Pierre decided to ask Jenny if she would spend a weekend in Paris with him as soon as he was on his feet again while Nat Phillips was visiting him and Jenny, furious, was tart with the young doctor, convinced that Nat would hurry straight back to his boss with this interesting titbit of information.

'So of course I went and told Pierre that I'd be in Paris anyway, doing modelling for a photographer, and that didn't please him. And then I said I would be working at Hyde Park Corner this afternoon, modelling rainwear, and that didn't please him either. Nat Phillips was all agog though!'

Sandra and Jenny were in the kitchen, making themselves a quick cup of tea, and now Sandra poured milk into the cups while Jenny tipped the pot and filled them. Sandra smiled and picked up the tea-tray.

'Poor old girl, you do get yourself into a pickle sometimes! Come on, we'll be devils and take this tea into the office and actually sit down to drink it. If I was off, I'd come and watch you dancing round Hyde Park myself, but unfortunately I'm on duty.'

'Good,' Jenny said, as they walked up the corridor. 'I hate being watched. Help, better hurry, someone's just gone into the office.'

They hurried to the office to find Janice Quinton waiting for them. She ignored Jenny but smiled graciously at Sandra.

'Ah, Sister, I've called for my wine; has it arrived, yet?'

Gillian's husband was clerk to a wine importer and could sometimes get good wine at very reasonable prices. Several members of the staff were glad to get their wine through him.

'No, but it's coming this afternoon,' Sandra said. 'How many bottles are you having? I'll get Monty to bring it down to your office, if you like.'

'Well, we've bought half-a-dozen but I was wondering if Monty could possibly bring it to my place? I'm off this afternoon, but I'll be home until three o'clock or so, if he could deliver it just for once? We're having a party tonight, so it would be nice if he could.'

Monty was a very obliging young man, and there was no doubt in Sandra's mind, Jenny could see, that he would deliver the wine.

'I'm sure he'll bring it round, only he won't know your address. Where shall I tell him? He'll probably be here at one, so you could have it at about half past.'

Janice, Jenny noticed, was smirking like a Cheshire cat and kept shooting little glances at Jenny. Odd!

'Oh yes, one-thirty will be fine. Tell him to bring it to seven, Chessington Mews. Got that?' She shot a malicious glance at Jenny. 'I'm sure Staff has!' She turned away from them, opened the door, and then turned back again for a moment. 'Tell Monty I'm eternally grateful and so will my . . . my fiancé be. I'd ask him in for a drink, only the wine is for the party.'

She left, her high heels clicking away down the corridor, and Sandra sank into her chair and began to sip her tea.

'Fiancé? That's a new name for it! Anyway, what did she mean by all that? What's the significance of

Chessington Mews?' She stared at Jenny. 'My dear child, you look sick; what is it?'

'It's Gerard Sterne's address,' Jenny said slowly. 'Well, it just goes to show you should never discount hospital gossip completely.' She drank her tea quickly, then stood up. 'I'm off, got to get cleared up so that I can go and be beautiful at Hyde Park Corner.'

But the remark had done all that Janice doubtless hoped it would. For the rest of the morning all Jenny could think about was Gerard and Janice living together. It was his business, his life, but she had thought him a very different kind of a man. Not the sort of man to pick up another's leavings, which Janice very definitely was. Everyone knew that she had very nearly wrecked Buckler's marriage, if not his career.

But work went on, and she was far too efficient and dedicated a nurse to let her sad and heavy thoughts affect her work. Sterne, she told herself, was just like all the others. He simply wanted a quiet life and a woman in his bed. At least he was not married, had no commitments. And if he really liked bottle-blondes with faces and natures like piranha fish . . . well, that was his concern.

I really don't care at all, she told herself as she tightened the cuff of the sphyg round Mr Selcott's arm. I could have had Mr Sterne and I didn't choose to, and it's as simple as that. I'm too young to get involved with a consultant, an important man. It was just that she missed his friendship, Jenny told herself. The truth was that he had come nearer than anyone else to making her want a permanent relationship, and she supposed that it was this she regretted.

Very soon, it would be time for his ward round, and she would be able to look at him and know that he really was living with Janice. That would probably give her sufficient incentive to be glad of her own escape!

And sure enough, any feelings she might have nurtured towards Gerard Sterne were soon completely lost beneath fury and outrage. He had been absolutely unbearable when he arrived and almost all his annoyance had been directed straight at her innocent and astonished head.

Why had she done this? Why had she not done that? Who was *she* to decide to change a patient's dosage without a doctor's consent? This, in Mr Selcott's very presence, was the final straw. Jenny cast aside her meek pose and glared angrily up at her tormentor.

'Mr Sterne, I've done no such thing and well you know it! The decision was Dr Anwalla's.'

'Really, Nurse Speed? Then where is the note to that effect?'

'There, sir.' She pointed. 'On top of the file.'

'I see. Then why is it in your handwriting?'

'Because Dr Anwalla asked me to write it to his dictation. His handwriting is very small and crabbed and the staff aren't used to it. He didn't want to risk a mistake.'

'Strange.' The word sounded like an accusation but before she could reply in kind, Mr Sterne had turned away from the bed and was striding, with his team following, out of the room. Over his shoulder he hurled a string of instructions.

'Suture removal . . . Arrange for sedation . . . Possibly it would be best in the circumstances to take him to theatre . . . Light anaesthetic . . . Speak to Dr Little . . .'

Jenny, hurrying along behind, was pleased when Nat Phillips dropped back too and gave her a wink.

'Sir's in a foul mood this morning, love,' he murmured. 'Don't worry, everyone's been getting it hot and
strong today.'

Jenny nodded and continued to follow the consultant,
but later, as she was hurrying to the canteen for her
lunch, Gerard Sterne came out of one of the ground
floor wards and called to her.

'Nurse! Here a minute.'

She hurried over to him and stood, hands clasped,
looking up at him. She did hope this would not mean
more trouble, more lectures!

'What's this about Paris?'

Immediately she felt hunted, on the defensive. What
had he heard? That Pierre had asked her to go there
for a weekend or that she was taking a two-day trip
there to do some modelling? Either, in his eyes, would
probably be equally blameworthy.

'Nothing's settled, yet.' she said. She stared down at
her shoes, determined not to meet his cross and accusing
eyes. 'It's only a thought at the moment.'

'Look, girl, you're going to bite off more than you
can chew. You'll live to regret all this independence,
you're . . .'

But Jenny, with an impatient exclamation, was
hurrying up the corridor, away from him. Glancing
over her shoulder, she called back, 'Yes, I'm sure
you're right, sir, only it's my lunch-break now . . .
can't wait . . .'

Nat Phillips, emerging from the ward just at the latter
part of this encounter, grinned at his boss's scarcely
concealed fury.

'It's no use, sir. It's her life and she's got to live it as
she sees fit. Anyway, why shouldn't she have a bit of a
fling with young Mongresin when he's better? Do them

both good, and she can always kick his kneecap if he gets bothersome.'

But Nat, in his turn, found himself talking to air. Gerard Sterne walked away from him, his head down, muttering.

The boss takes it too far, Dr Phillips thought as he set off down the corridor in Sterne's wake. All this interference in a young nurse's love life could only be construed as unnecessary, unless . . .

Nat Phillips stared. Unless that little fling that Sterne had indulged in earlier with the girl had been a lot more serious than anyone had dreamed!

'Face into the wind, darling, and try not to wince! Think *figurehead*! Perfect, don't smile, don't move . . .' Click, click, click, click went the camera, punctuating Ralph's remarks.

Jenny, thinking figurehead and refraining from even the tiniest smile, sighed and wished the wind would drop and wondered why nursing had seemed such hard work and modelling so easy. Right now she would have given a good deal for a warm ward and the prospect of a quick cuppa. Instead here she was, facing into a force eight gale, not allowed to smile or screw up her face even though her eyes were full of tears and wind-whipped eyelashes, with goosepimples all over her bare legs and a secret conviction that someone was pouring ice-cold water down her cleavage.

Glamorous? Exciting? Not on your life! But it was well paid and she did so want a car of her own!

'Right, darling, we'll call it a day.' Ralph, who might be conceited and far too handsome for his own good, nevertheless had a streak of humanity somewhere, Jenny conceded as he accompanied his words by cuddling his own thick coat around her. 'You're like an icicle, woman. Going to let me take you out to dinner tonight?'

'Thanks very much Ralph, but . . .' Even the thought of discussing Paris was not sufficiently alluring, right now, to let herself get caught in Ralph's experienced grasp. Other models had passed the word around that Ralph expected generous recompense for a good dinner, and she was not up to fighting anyone off, cold and tired as she was.

'Not tonight? Then how about tomorrow night? I'll take you somewhere glamorous and we'll talk about this Paris trip. I take it you do want to come along? The money's good and I've told Netta I want you if you're available. We can choose the time to suit you.'

As this moment, with the remark ringing in her ears, Jenny glanced across at the audience that a session with a photographer always seems to collect and there was Gerard Sterne, with Janice hanging on to his arm. He was not looking at her right now but down at Janice, and his expression was impatient, the set of his mouth grim. Jenny had been about to refuse Ralph's invitation and to explain that her agent would settle the details with him when she saw the couple and, immediately, it became important to let Gerard see how comfortable she was, how wooed by fashionable young photographers, how far from needing him!

'Tomorrow would be marvellous, darling,' she said as loudly and clearly as she could. 'I just hope you'll take me somewhere really special!'

She glanced up at Ralph, who had an arm slung carelessly round her shoulders, and surprised a complex expression on his face. Amazement, because she had never responded to his blandishments before, delight, because she had just done so, and a sort of smug and anticipatory look, too. It was the look of a gourmet who has often longed to taste a certain dish and now sees that the opportunity to do so has arisen.

Oh dear, Jenny thought apprehensively, what have I done now? I really must make sure that this particular dish goes untasted tomorrow evening! But she was still acting largely to impress Gerard and Janice, so she smiled lovingly at Ralph and climbed into the taxi he had hailed, cooing, 'Until tomorrow, darling,' as she waved out of the window.

Later, thinking it over, Jenny decided she had done rather well on two scores. Firstly, Gerard would realise that she was most definitely not pining for him. And secondly, the word would probably get around to Pierre that she had another interest beside himself. She did not want to hurt Pierre, but neither did she want to find herself bound to go out with him just because of his injuries.

It was odd, in view of her feelings, that Jenny still felt no real satisfaction with herself as she lay in a hot bath later that night, with a big bath towel warming on the rail and an expensive box of talcum waiting to be generously puffed all over her. In fact, apprehension was beginning to rear its ugly head. If she could land the modelling job she would probably be able to buy that car. Then she could drive off into the sunset, alone, if that was what she wanted. But before then, there was dinner and an evening with Ralph to be got through. She cursed her own stupidity in saying she would go. But still, he could scarcely eat her in a restaurant, and she would make it very plain that she intended to take herself home alone and unpawed.

If she went to Paris, of course, she would presumably

spend all the time when she wasn't working fighting Ralph off. Or would she? No, on second thoughts. Since there were to be three models, she could easily find Ralph smitten with one of the others, and that would be very nice.

Her mind, free from apprehension on that score, turned to other things, and before she could stop it she realised she was thinking about Gerard, in his lovely little house, holding Janice in his arms, raining kisses on her eager little piranha mouth. Rather than think about such a repellent business she leapt out of the bath, scattering hot water and bath oil all over the lino, and began towelling herself vigorously.

Damn Gerard and damn Janice . . . I wonder whether the Paris trip would run to a Porsche, she asked herself. But then there was insurance, and running costs . . . Would he cuddle Janice in the car, on their way home? And of course, there would be parking. Perhaps a Mini would be best, after all. If Janice sat on his knee as they watched telly in the evenings she would probably fracture his femur, and that would serve him right!

Jenny threw on her dressing-gown and hurried out of the bathroom. I will not think about them, she told herself fiercely, snatching up a book and opening it at random. I will *not* think about them!

CHAPTER NINE

NEXT DAY Mr Selcott's sutures were removed in theatre and he was brought back to his room. Jenny saw him into bed and then brought her coffee through so that she would be with him when he came properly round. She checked that he was a good colour and that the stump, neatly covered with Rayolast bandaging, was lying still and apparently not giving any trouble, then she sat down in her chair to wait for him to wake. He was doing well and actually looking forward, he said, to the fitting of his artificial limb.

'Morning, Nurse.' Mr Sterne, still in theatre greens, came into the room and closed the door softly behind him. 'The wound has healed well, couldn't be better. All well here?'

'Yes, sir. He isn't round yet, which is why I've brought my coffee through.'

'Good, good.' Mr Sterne walked over to the window and spoke with his back to her. 'I want a word with you, as it happens.'

'Carry on, sir.'

There was little else she could say, Jenny thought despairingly, as he turned from the window and came to stand directly in front of her, his dark eyes fixed on hers.

'I saw you yesterday, when you were being photographed in the park. That man . . . Jenny, are you out of your mind? Predatory isn't the word. He's the sort with only one use for a woman! I know you saw me, so don't widen your eyes like that, and try to look innocent!

If he takes you out to dinner tonight, if you go to Paris with him . . . Well, you know what will happen, don't you?' She did not answer. 'Look, is that what you *want*, dammit? I've always thought you a sensible girl, but surely you can see what sort he is? That fellow?'

'I can handle it,' Jenny said unsteadily. Her heart was singing because she could hear genuine concern in his voice. Not that it meant anything, she reminded herself, but it was good to hear!

'You, handle him! It's no business of mine, I've other worries, my own life to live, but you can no more handle a man of his experience than you could have handled me, if I'd tried . . .'

'I could handle that sort of thing whoever tried it,' Jenny said hotly. Fancy Mr Sterne daring to insinuate that he could have overcome her resistance if he had wanted to do so! It was damned insulting, and that was putting it pretty mildly. 'I appreciate your concern, Mr Sterne, but it's unnecessary. I know exactly how to deal with Ralph, and if you're worried that a trip to Paris will interfere with my nursing, I can assure you I'll go in my own time and not the hospital's.'

'I'm not worried about your work, that's excellent, I admit it. Look, Jenny, forget you hate me for a moment . . .'

'I don't hate you! Only you thought I was a liar, you believed a lot of rubbish about me—you can't blame me for not trusting you any more!'

'If you can't trust me you can't trust anyone! I'm very much your friend, I've got your welfare very much at heart, and I'm telling you that Melville's trouble! You won't be able to keep him off if he's determined, and Paris can be a lonely city for a girl by herself. Jenny, tell him no!'

'I can handle it, I tell you!' Jenny was nearly shouting in her attempt to convince him. 'I can manage Ralph easily and anyway, it's a very well paid job. I need the money, I don't see why I shouldn't go to Paris and do some work and get paid without having you down on me!'

'I see; some girls would think the price might be too high.' His eyes were hot with anger but his voice was cold. 'Don't forget you're supposed to be selling your services in front of the camera and not in some sordid little hotel bedroom!'

Jenny jumped. Her fury knew no bounds. How dared he!

'That's enough! If I want to go to the devil I'll go without any help from you! How dare you tell me what to do as if you were a plaster saint when everyone knows you're living with a nasty little trollop who isn't fit to clean bedpans!'

'Wha . . . *What* did you say? Just come here . . .'

But Jenny decided that she had gone too far. There was a white line round Gerard Sterne's mouth and his fists showed whitened knuckles. She whisked round and made for the door. Behind her, she heard him start across the room and neither paused nor looked back, not even when she heard Mr Selcott say something in a dreamy, low voice. She flew down the corridor and shot into the sluice where Pat was arranging roses in a crystal vase. She raised her eyes in surprise at Jenny's abrupt arrival.

'Hello, what's biting you? Devil on your tail? Just look at these roses! They're for Patrice Carruthers and all she's in for is bed-rest. I wish someone would send me three dozen roses and a heart-shaped box of hand-made chocolates every time I lay in bed!'

'Don't we all,' whispered Jenny, with a hunted glance over her shoulder. If only he would go away now, and leave her alone! Her heart was hammering nineteen to the dozen and she longed to be by herself so that she could indulge in a good cry. He thought her capable of selling herself for a well-paid job, he told her off, he shouted at her . . . And fool that I am, I love him, she started to think, but the ending of the sentence brought her up short. Loved him? How could she love someone who was so hateful, who believed the worst of her all the time and who was living with the nastiest woman in the hospital into the bargain? But Jenny was nothing if not practical. She had not known she loved him until she had recognised and acknowledged the concern in his voice, but then it had burst upon her in all its glory. He was not worthy of her love, he was bossy and cruel and self-satisfied, but that could not kill the feeling, though she knew it to be foolish.

Perhaps it would go away, she told herself without much conviction, as she helped Pat with the roses. Perhaps it would fade beneath the harsh light of his affection for Janice and his eventual indifference to herself. It had proved a resilient little plant so far though, having struggled on through the miserable time when he had believed her to be lying to get herself out of trouble, refusing to be killed off by his withering nastiness over Pierre, over almost everything she did.

'There, finished,' Pat said with satisfaction, when every bloom was in place. 'Come on, Jenny, there's another fellow due up from theatre in about five minutes.'

The door, opening at that point, almost sent Jenny into rigor. She froze, not daring to turn her head.

'Oh, you're here.' It was Sandra's voice, calm,

untroubled. 'Jenny, what have you been up to this time? Sterne wants to see you in his office first thing tomorrow.'

Jenny turned and heaved a huge sigh.

'Oh damn, and I suppose I'll have to turn up. He's annoyed with me for taking the Paris job.'

She and Sandra left the room together. Sandra raised quizzical brows at her.

'Yes, he mentioned something of the sort. Jenny, Sterne isn't usually a bit interested in the private lives of his staff; do you think . . .?'

'I don't know what to think,' Jenny said sombrely. 'Let's leave it until after I've seen him tomorrow, Sandy.'

'Well, love? Shall you come back to my place or shall we go back to yours?'

Ralph and Jenny, having eaten an excellent meal, drunk some very good wine and settled all the details of the Paris trip, were climbing into a taxi. Jenny felt relaxed and comfortable. Ralph had been charming, a good companion and an interesting one as well. He had made the Paris trip sound a treat too good to be missed as well as a generously paid assignment. So now Jenny made no objection as he put a casual arm round her shoulders and snuggled her up.

'I have to go home, please, Ralph. I'm very tired, but it's been a marvellous evening and thank you very much. I can't ask you in though, because I share with three other nurses and there really isn't room, what with them washing their hair and hanging their tights all over the place.'

'Right, home it shall be. The address?'

Jenny gave him the address of the modern block of

flats on Byron Road. She thought, guiltily, that he had not pressed for an invitation to visit her flat because he was sure that she would be more than willing to accept his proposals in Paris. Really she should disillusion him before the trip. Otherwise, as Mr Sterne had said, she could have quite a nasty time in the French capital. The fact that Ralph had known her for three years and had always appeared to accept the fact that she did not want affairs would not be enough to expect good behaviour, she knew that. After all, she was a nurse now, and men often had very odd ideas about nurses. She supposed, vaguely, that it was something to do with all those beds.

His behaviour in the taxi was rather amorous, too. His hands seemed to be everywhere, his mouth nuzzled at her neck, his fingers clawed at her green silk dress. Altogether, she was more than a little relieved when the taxi stopped beside the kerb and she saw the familiar flats on her right. Rather breathlessly she extricated herself from Ralph's octopus embrace.

'Thanks for a lovely evening, Ralph. Look, I haven't changed in the past few years, you know. I still feel just like I did when we worked together last.' She got out of the taxi and, rather to her dismay, he followed her, putting a heavy arm round her shoulders and drawing her close. 'Ralph, I'm sorry, but . . .'

His mouth opened, then covered hers. Jenny found herself disliking the experience more and more. She pushed his chest, then kicked out and managed to move away from him. He was breathing heavily and he laughed a little breathlessly, then looped an arm round her waist and drew her close, though he seemed content for the moment just to hold her.

'Dear little Jenny! You don't want to play now, right? Until Paris, then.'

Jenny took a deep breath and tried not to notice the way his eyes slid hotly over her figure in the suddenly fragile green silk.

'I don't sleep around, Ralph. Not with anyone or for any reason.'

'What do you mean? Why, you little! You must have known I wouldn't take a girl to Paris unless . . .'

'Oh grow up, Ralph!' Jenny's voice was sharp with contempt. She turned away from him, stalking with dignity under the darkness of the arch and through its tunnel-like length into the courtyard in the middle of the block.

Damn, damn, and damn again. She would have to ring Netta tomorrow and tell her the Paris trip was off, but perhaps it was for the best. Fancy not discovering Ralph's intentions until he was climbing into her bed! Her hair rose on her head at the thought. No, she would not go to Paris, and she would get as much ordinary work as she could instead, and then she would have earned her little car by the sweat of her brow, rather than by a lucky break.

Outside, in the road, she heard the taxi drive off. She waited a moment and then, judging it safe to emerge once more, she left the moonlit courtyard and walked back, into the darkness of the tunnel.

She was actually about to step into the lamplit street once more when the arms went round her waist, dragging her back into the thick darkness.

For a moment, oddly enough, she thought it was a joke; that it was one of the girls fooling about, or even one of the chaps from the arcade, intent on giving her a scare. And for that moment she neither screamed nor struggled. She just gasped, then tried to turn and see who it was who held her.

Then the grip on her waist told her that it was no joke; this was an attack in deadly earnest. No one was going to say, 'Idiot!' in a loud and cheerful voice as they released her. Her shoulder-bag was torn from her grip and just as it crossed her mind that she was being robbed, she heard it strike the ground some way off and knew that whoever held her wanted her and not her pitifully small supply of money. She drew in her breath for a scream and a hand gagged her, then she was hit violently across the head and thrown so hard on to the ground that all the breath was knocked out of her and for a moment she could only lie there, gasping for air, powerless to move a muscle.

The man fell on his knees beside her with a grunt and grabbed at the front of her dress. It ripped easily at his onslaught, and then he was on her, they were fighting in earnest, with Jenny, her breath and courage returning, kicking, biting, clawing, and trying to shriek whenever her mouth was free from that hateful, gagging hand.

Then the fingers closed round her throat.

'One scream and I'll strangle you,' the voice said softly, and the fingers tightened in dreadful warning.

Jenny lay still for a moment, gathering all her strength and courage. Then she felt him relax and move across her and at the same moment she kicked out with all her strength and felt her knee connect with a satisfying crunch.

Her attacker gave a hoarse shriek and fell sideways, and then Jenny was on her feet, winged feet it seemed, and flying as fast and as far from the archway as she possibly could. She heard a fumbling step, saw, out of the corner of her eye, the man's dark shape lurching, injured . . . But she had no time for conjecture, no time for anything but running, putting as much distance as possible between herself and those strangling hands. She ran and ran, holding her dress together with scratched and bleeding fingers, past the quiet little streets, the closed and darkened shops, wanting lights, people, help.

The hospital. There it was, brightly lit, comfortingly familiar, with people moving about inside and friends who would take care of her.

She got to the big doors which led into Casualty and was through them and standing, swaying, in the brightly lit foyer. She saw someone in nurses' uniform, took an uncertain step forward, and blackness rushed up to meet her.

Voices. Soft, concerned. Hands on her face, hands on her bruised legs . . . Jenny came round and sat up, eyes black with terror, a scream ready to hand, to find herself sitting on an examination couch in Casualty with Helen's bright hair and concerned face near, and a young, dark-haired doctor talking earnestly to a police constable.

'Jenny, you've come round!' Considering that she had just sat up like a jack-in-the-box, this must be the understatement of the year, Jenny thought, but she said nothing, only putting out a trembling hand and grabbing Helen's wrist. Helen patted her soothingly. 'It's all right, my love, you're safe. The policeman would like to know what happened, though.'

The policeman smiled reassuringly at Jenny.

'All right, Miss? Can you tell us what happened?'

Haltingly, Jenny explained about the dark passage, the man who had grabbed her, and her missing handbag.

'Hmm.' The policeman spoke into a small receiver set and was heard to send someone off to Byron Road flats. 'Sharpish,' he concluded, and then turned back to Jenny. 'Your handbag's there, you think? Then you weren't attacked for money?'

'I don't know. He tried to strangle me,' Jenny muttered. She put her hands up to her bruised throat. 'He threw my bag away but he may have meant to go back for it later.'

'Any idea who it may have been?'

Jenny's conscience might balk at getting an innocent man into trouble, but it would be easy enough to be sure that he *was* innocent after their fight. If Ralph was unmarked then it had not been he who had attacked her.

'I wonder whether it was the chap who'd taken me out for the evening? Ralph Melville. He's a successful photographer. He'll be in the yellow pages.'

The policeman nodded and spoke once more into his radio.

'Right, love, that's all for now. The doctor here wants to give you a good going over, make sure everything's in working order, and then I think you'd best go home and straight to bed.' He was only a young man, but his smile was fatherly, understanding. 'If you think of anything else, just let us know in the morning.'

'Right, officer,' Jenny said. She waited until he had gone and then gave the young casualty officer the benefit of what she hoped was a stern glare. 'I'm perfectly all right. Nothing happened . . . if you see what I mean.'

He caught Helen's eye. 'Nurse, if you wouldn't mind . . .' Ten minutes later he called Helen back through the curtains.

'All right?' Helen squeezed Jenny's hand as she climbed off the couch and stood for a moment, swaying, trying to adjust herself to being on her feet once more. 'Look, you'd better have a taxi home.'

'Yes, perhaps I'd better.' Jenny moved across to the foyer, then stopped short, a hand flying to her mouth. 'Mercy, my front door key was in the handbag!'

'You can borrow . . .'

'Nurse! Would you come here, please?'

Helen, seeing Sister trying to cope with a very large, very drunk man in bus-driver's uniform, shook Jenny's arm.

'I've got to go, but take my key and some money for the taxi out of my handbag. And get a good night's sleep!'

The young casualty officer, hovering, watched while Jenny found the bag and extracted the money and the key, and then he took her arm.

'I'll get you a taxi, it won't take . . .'

Mr Sterne came striding across the foyer and stopped short at the sight of Jenny, pale and distressed still, hugging a borrowed cardigan across the front of her ripped dress.

'Hallo, what's all this? Can I help?'

'I'm just getting Nurse Speed a taxi, sir,' the young doctor said quickly. 'But actually I'm on call. If you're on your way out do you think you could see her safely into a cab?'

Mr Sterne came over and put a proprietorial hand on her elbow.

'I'm finished for tonight, so I'll give her a lift.' He did not wait to be thanked but propelled Jenny out ahead of him, into the darkness. 'Come along, young woman, you look as if you've been in a fight and lost. Let's get you home.'

Jenny found herself ensconced in the car with no very clear idea of how she got there. She stole a glance at Mr Sterne's profile; nice, clean, dependable. She swallowed a small sob. Just wait until he knew what this was all about. How he would love reminding her that he had told her so!

It was not far to the flat; this time, she let him drive her right up to the amusement arcade, though it was shuttered and quiet now. She sat very still when the car stopped by the kerb, suddenly feeling sure that her knees were too weak to hold her. She began to speak, then stopped. She knew that she could not get out of the warmth and safety of this car and go across the pavement and up the stairs into the lonely flat. Helen and Katrina were both away tonight, but it was not the loneliness which bothered her. It was the fact that the key had been in her handbag—and *he* could be up there by now, waiting for her, ready to pounce, to finish off what he had started in the tunnel under the flats.

'Would you like me to come up with you? Jenny, what's happened to you? I thought back there in the hospital that you'd fallen off a bus or been grazed by a passing car or something.' A hand took her chin gently, turning her to face him. 'Jenny? Come on, sweetheart, what is it?'

'I was attacked and my handbag was stolen,' Jenny said slowly. 'Gerard, I'm scared. Suppose the thief took my key? Suppose he's hiding in the flat now, waiting for me?'

His arm went round her shoulders, hugging her to him. He was warmth, security.

'Now how should a chance-met sneak thief know which is your flat? And anyway, what about your flatmates? They'll come down if you ring.'

Jenny shook her head and cuddled closer.

'No. Helen's on nights, Katrina's staying with her cousin and Mandy's on leave. And I think the . . . the man knew it was me.'

'I see.' Gerard took his arm from around her and leaned forward to turn the ignition key. The engine purred into life. 'Then there's only one thing for it. You'll have to stay in my spare room for a night.'

Greatly to her own surprise, Jenny made not the slightest demur. Relief was too warm and sweet. She just leaned back in the seat and closed her eyes and let the feeling flood over her. To stay with Gerard! To know that no one would find her there, no one would come stealing up the stairs to try to strangle her. Not even to herself would she admit what her attacker's ultimate aim must have been.

They reached the Mews and were at the door before Jenny remembered Janice. She clutched Gerard's arm.

'Won't Janice mind?' she said anxiously. 'I don't want to get anyone into trouble.'

'Janice? My secretary?' He propelled her ahead of him up the stairs to the small hall at the top. 'Why on earth should she mind if you spend the night in my spare room?'

They entered the kitchen and Jenny flopped on to a chair. Far too tired and upset to dissemble, she said miserably, 'Well, she's living with you, she said so this afternoon. She said her wine had better be delivered here, since you and she were giving a party. And everyone knows you're lovers, anyway.'

'Oh, everyone knows, do they?' He put the kettle on and lit the gas, then turned back to her. He was smiling. 'Janice was pulling your leg, my love. The only woman who has ever lived with me in this house is Isabel and the wine was mine, paid for by me but delivered to this place by Janice since she had the afternoon off. I'll swear to that on a whole stack of Bibles, if it will make you happier. Now I'm going to make you a hot chocolate laced with rum and then you're going to tell me exactly what happened tonight.'

Presently, with half her rum and hot chocolate warming her and the other half still in the mug waiting to be drunk, the two of them sat side by side on the big, soft couch in the living-room and Jenny began to come out of her state of shock. She sipped her drink and felt contentment flood through her. She was in Gerard's house, sitting close to him, and of the detestable Miss Quinton there was no sign whatsoever. Tomorrow he might be Mr Sterne again, the angry, unpredictable consultant, but now he was just dear Gerard, who would look after her.

'Come on then, Jenny, tell me the whole story right from the beginning and don't leave anything out. Remember Baby!'

She had thought she could never tell anyone all that awful experience, but it was easy to tell Gerard. She even admitted that she believed her attacker had been Ralph Melville. And then she was generous.

'You don't have to tell me it was my own fault, Gerard, because I know it was. I should have listened to you when you kept warning me, but I couldn't admit, even to myself, that I was making a foolish mistake. So I got what I deserved, I suppose.'

She heard him mutter something and then he turned and took her in his arms. His breath was warm on her hair as he started to speak.

'Jenny, if the fault was anyone's, it was mine! Every time I got a chance to speak to you I wanted to beg you to let me take care of you, protect you against people like Melville, but my wretched pride didn't dare risk a rebuff. So instead I warned you, tried to dictate what you should and should not do, and never once risked telling you the truth. You wouldn't even come out with me and I was convinced by then that you hated me and

wanted someone younger, like Mongresin. What a fool
I was—and what harm I could have done, just because
I wouldn't tell you I loved you for fear you'd become
even colder and more remote!'

'Me? Cold and remote? Oh, Gerard, how could you!'
Jenny turned in the circle of his arm and kissed him as
passionately as the circumstances permitted. He
groaned against her mouth, returning the kiss every bit
as hotly, then held her back from him, smiling with a
certain complacence.

'Jenny? Do you love me?'

'Oh, I do,' Jenny sighed, snuggling closer. 'But you
didn't seem to like me a bit! You snarled at me and
criticised and scolded, and you were horrible about poor
Pierre and you pretended to believe all the things Mr
Whelpton said . . .'

'That was jealousy,' Gerard said smugly, as though
even jealousy was now something to boast about. 'I
didn't believe Douglas Whelpton, but it was like an
aching tooth. I kept biting on it and driving myself into
a fury by telling myself that you were unworthy of love.'

'Oh, charming!' Jenny took his hand and bit his
fingers gently. 'So if I hadn't been attacked tonight I
suppose you'd never have said anything to me and we'd
have gone our separate ways?'

'Not a chance! I made up my mind this very day,
when you shot out of Selcott's room and disappeared,
that I'd got to take my chance. I fully intended to ask
you to marry me tomorrow morning, when you came
to my office.' He kissed her softly, with little kisses,
across her cheek and rounded chin. 'If I hadn't, I think
Mr Selcott would have blown the gaffe! After you'd
left, he told me a thing or two—how you were the best
nurse and the prettiest girl in the hospital, how faint

heart never won fair lady . . . Dear me, a catalogue of excellent advice which I fully intended to take.'

'Golly, marriage,' Jenny sighed, leaning back and surveying the surgeon through half-closed lids. 'But I can't marry until I'm twenty-five, Gerard, I've vowed I won't, and that's not for another four years.'

Gerard scooped her into his arms and stood up. He was smiling, but there was something about the set of his mouth and the flare of his nostrils which made Jenny's heart thump a little harder in her breast.

'I'm sorry, sweetheart, but I'm not prepared to wait four years. I want you far too much for that. So what's it to be? Agreement or unfair persuasion? Because we Sternes stop at nothing to get what we want!'

Jenny threw both her arms round his neck and began to kiss him. Between kisses she spoke.

'Oh well, in that case, the answer's . . . Yes!'

He gave a triumphant laugh and then stepped back, swayed, and the two of them fell heavily on to the couch. Jenny, finding herself pulled back into his arms once more, began to speak and then gave up any attempt at rational conversation. It was plainly useless, he was not listening!

'Gerard, I do love you so much . . . and mind my drinking chocolate!'

Mr Sterne's foot caught the half-full mug and drinking chocolate spread, puddled, and began to seep into the deep pile of the carpet. Isabel, who had been hiding behind the couch while all the talking and kissing went on, came out and settled herself comfortably beside the delectable pool of milky chocolate. In the silence, she began, delicately, to lap it up.

Mills & Boon

4 Doctor Nurse Romances
FREE

Coping with the daily tragedies and ordeals of a busy hospital, and sharing the satisfaction of a difficult job well done, people find themselves unexpectedly drawn together. Mills & Boon Doctor Nurse Romances capture perfectly the excitement, the intrigue and the emotions of modern medicine, that so often lead to overwhelming and blissful love. By becoming a regular reader of Mills & Boon Doctor Nurse Romances you can enjoy EIGHT superb new titles every two months plus a whole range of special benefits: your very own personal membership card, a free newsletter packed with recipes, competitions, bargain book offers, plus big cash savings.

**AND an Introductory FREE GIFT for YOU.
Turn over the page for details.**

Fill in and send this coupon back today
and we'll send you
4 Introductory
Doctor Nurse Romances yours to keep
FREE

At the same time we will reserve a
subscription to Mills & Boon
Doctor Nurse Romances for you. Every
two months you will receive the latest
8 new titles, delivered direct to your door.
You don't pay extra for delivery. Postage and
packing is always completely Free.
There is no obligation or commitment –
you receive books only for
as long as you want to.

**It's easy! Fill in the coupon below and return it to
MILLS & BOON READER SERVICE, FREEPOST, P.O. BOX 236,
CROYDON, SURREY CR9 9EL.**

**Please note: READERS IN SOUTH AFRICA write to
Mills & Boon Ltd., Postbag X3010,
Randburg 2125, S. Africa.**

- -

FREE BOOKS CERTIFICATE

**To: Mills & Boon Reader Service, FREEPOST, P.O. Box 236,
Croydon, Surrey CR9 9EL.**

Please send me, free and without obligation, four Dr. Nurse Romances, and reserve a
Reader Service Subscription for me. If I decide to subscribe I shall receive, following my free
parcel of books, eight new Dr. Nurse Romances every two months for £8.00, post and
packing free. If I decide not to subscribe, I shall write to you within 10 days. The free books
are mine to keep in any case. I understand that I may cancel my subscription at any time
simply by writing to you. I am over 18 years of age.
Please write in BLOCK CAPITALS.

Name _____

Address _____

_____

_____ Postcode _____

SEND NO MONEY — TAKE NO RISKS

Remember, postcodes speed delivery. Offer applies in UK only and is not valid to
present subscribers. Mills & Boon reserve the right to exercise discretion
in granting membership. If price changes are necessary you will be noti-
fied. Offer expires 30th June 1985.

8DN

EP

certain I was in love with Shona, that I'd not allowed myself to see what was happening to me.'

His eyes were very dark, as he waited for her to speak.

'And what was happening to you, Ross?' Karen asked, not quite steadily.

'My own lass,' Ross said, and his voice was unsteady too, 'you must know that I was falling in love with you.'

And if she needed anything more to convince her, he took her in his arms, and his lips were warm and demanding on hers. A demand that she could meet now with no reservations, with nothing held back, because she knew at last that he loved her as strongly and as surely as she had loved him for all this waiting time.

While away the lazy days of late Summer with our new gift selection
Intimate Moments

Four Romances, new in paperback, from four favourite authors.
The perfect treat!

The Colour of the Sea
Rosemary Hammond

Had We Never Loved
Jeneth Murrey

The Heron Quest
Charlotte Lamb

Magic of the Baobab
Yvonne Whittal

Available from July 1991. Price: £6.40

Available from Boots, Martins, John Menzies, W.H. Smith, Woolworths
and other paperback stockists.

Also available from Mills and Boon Reader Service,
P.O. Box 236, Thornton Road, Croydon, Surrey CR9 3RU.

COMING IN SEPTEMBER

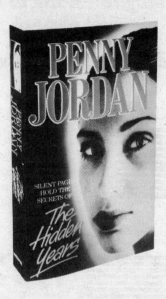

The eagerly awaited new novel from this internationally bestselling author. Lying critically injured in hospital, Liz Danvers implores her estranged daughter to return home and read her diaries. As Sage reads she learns of painful secrets in her mothers hidden past, and begins to feel compassion and a reluctant admiration for this woman who had stood so strongly between herself and the man she once loved. The diaries held the clues to a number of emotional puzzles, but the biggest mystery of all was why Liz had chosen to reveal her most secret life to the one person who had every reason to resent and despise her.

Available: September 1991. Price £4.99

W**O**RLDWIDE

From: Boots, Martins, John Menzies, W.H. Smith,
Woolworths and other paperback stockists.
Also available from Reader Service, Thornton Road,
Croydon Surrey, CR9 3RU